SCARLETT UNDERCOVER

JENNIFER LATHAM

LITTLE, BROWN AND COMPANY
New York · Boston

Little, Brown and Company

Hachette Book Group
1290 Avenue of the Americas, New York, NY 10104
Visit us at lb-teens.com

Little, Brown and Company is a division of Hachette Book Group, Inc. The Little, Brown name and logo are trademarks of Hachette Book Group, Inc.

The publisher is not responsible for websites (or their content) that are not owned by the publisher.

First Paperback Edition: November 2016
First published in hardcover in May 2015 by Little, Brown and Company

The Library of Congress has cataloged the hardcover edition as follows:

Latham, Jennifer.
Scarlett undercover / Jennifer Latham.
pages cm
Summary: "Scarlett, a sixteen-year-old private detective in the fictional city of Las Almas, finds herself at the center of a mysterious case—involving ancient curses, priceless artifacts, and jinn—as she discovers that her own family secrets may have more to do with the situation than she thinks"—Provided by publisher.
ISBN 978-0-316-28393-9 (hardcover)—ISBN 978-0-316-28389-2 (ebook)—ISBN 978-0-316-28395-3 (library edition ebook) [1. Private investigators—Fiction. 2. Supernatural—Fiction. 3. Blessing and cursing—Fiction. 4. Genies—Fiction. 5. Secrets—Fiction. 6. Mystery and detective stories.] I. Title.
PZ7.L3483Sc 2015
[Fic]—dc23   2014013252

Paperback ISBN 978-0-316-28394-6

10 9 8 7 6 5 4 3 2 1

LSC-C

Printed in the United States of America

For Sean, Zoë, and Sophie

Because my own story wouldn't be worth
telling if it wasn't for you.

Do not be satisfied with the stories that come before you. Unfold your own myth.

—Jalal ad-Din Muhammad Rumi

1

The kid was cute. Her bare, knobbly legs swung back and forth like pendulums between the chipped legs of my client chair. Plastic safety goggles rested on her forehead, held tight by an elastic band that circled her head and pooched her bobbed brown hair up at the crown. She was thin. Delicate, even. But her eyes were clear and blue and smart.

"I think my brother killed someone."

It was a hell of a thing to say, especially for someone who'd just walked into my office wearing a pale pink jumper only a mother could love. I waited for her to keep talking. She didn't.

"How about you tell me your name before we get into that?" I said.

"Gemma Archer. My brother's Oliver." Her hands twisted the strap of her bag.

"Nice to meet you, Gemma. I'm Scarlett."

She nodded like she already knew that. Which, of course, she did.

"Okay. Now, exactly who do you think your brother killed?"

"His friend Quinn Johnson," she said in a voice flat as truck stop pancakes.

The name sounded familiar, but I couldn't place it.

"He's the boy they pulled out of Las Almas Bay yesterday. The one who jumped off the Baker Street Bridge," she said quietly.

Things clicked into place. I'd just read about Quinn Johnson's death in the paper that morning. The thing was, it hadn't been murder; it'd been a suicide. I looked over at the half-eaten bagel on my desk. My stomach grumbled.

"Well, kid," I said, "I don't think you need me. Two witnesses saw your brother's friend jump off that bridge all on his own. It's an awful mess, and I'm sorry for him and his family and anyone who knew him. But your brother wasn't even there."

"You're wrong," she said. "Oliver might not have been with Quinn when he died, but that doesn't mean he wasn't responsible."

It had happened before—me being wrong, that is. So I shrugged and played along.

"How old's your brother?"

"Fifteen."

"And what makes you think he had anything to do with the Johnson kid's death?"

She chewed her lip, looked around like she wished she could disappear into the walls.

"He's all dark, like a light went out inside him."

I told her she'd have to be a little more specific than that.

"I don't know. He's just…*dark!* And he doesn't talk to me or see me or play his guitar anymore. He cleans his room now, too, and mostly only comes home to eat. Then, when he *is* home, he won't put his phone down. I thought he was on it a lot before, but it's crazy lately."

She got quiet again.

"Look, kid," I said. "I'm not one to turn down a job, but it doesn't sound like there's much I can do for you. Have you talked to your parents about all this?"

Her shoulders slumped, and a soft little hiccup hitched in her throat.

"I tried." She didn't bother to wipe away the tear slipping down her cheek. "They won't listen. No one will."

I dug deep and found my patient voice. "Don't you think your parents would have noticed if your brother was in trouble?"

"My parents don't notice anything," she whispered.

That got me. Right in the gut.

"People change, kid," I said, softening. "And your brother must be pretty messed up after what happened to his friend."

She looked lost. Her mouth trembled. Her head shook back and forth.

"But he's not! Not even a little! That's the problem. Plus I saw him and Quinn together in the courtyard after school last week and..."

Her voice faded to nothing. Her shoulders shook.

"And what? What happened?"

She paused. Gathered herself.

"I was up by the gate and only heard a little. Quinn said, 'We can't let them,' and Oliver said something I couldn't hear. Then Quinn..."

She looked up at me like she wasn't sure she should go on. I gave her my best encouraging smile. She took a deep breath.

"He said, 'Eff you and eff the rest of them, too. You're all crazy.'"

"Only he didn't say *eff*, right? He said the *F* word?" She nodded.

"What did your brother do then?"

She looked at her hands. Sniffled.

"Gemma?"

"He said, 'Tell us where he is, or we'll kill you and Sam both.'"

"And you don't know who *he* is?"

"No."

"Who's Sam?"

"Quinn's little brother."

"What happened next?"

"Quinn punched him."

"They fought?"

"No." She shook her head. "Oliver just smiled. And even though his mouth was bleeding, he pulled his finger across his throat real slow, like he was threatening to kill Quinn. Then he walked away."

"Where was Oliver when Quinn went to the bridge?"

"At home. But it's like I said, for the last few weeks he's been all dead inside. I know he didn't actually *push* Quinn, but if it weren't for Oliver, I don't think Quinn would have jumped."

I sat back in my chair and laced my fingers together behind my head.

"You know, there's no guarantee I'll find anything if I take the case. And even if I do, you might not like it."

"I've got money." She pulled a wad of cash the size of a melon out of her backpack. "What else am I supposed to spend this on?"

A long list of things came to mind, but I kept them to myself. That's me. Always thinking.

I leaned forward and folded my hands on the desk. "How about I chew on this awhile and get back to you?"

Gemma's lips quivered, but she kept it together.

"I just want my real brother back," she said. Then she gave me her number and walked herself to the door.

"I'll call you," I said.

She didn't stop. Just dropped her chin and kept on walking.

A couple of hours later, my breakfast was long gone, and Gemma was still on my mind. Rain pattered against the window behind me. Tires swished on Carroll Street's wet pavement two stories below. On any given weekday it would have been busy down there, full of people with places to go. But at eleven o'clock on a gray Saturday morning, the only soul out was the General, peeing against a Dumpster in the alley across the street. He was the cheerful kind of neighborhood drunk who'd tip his hat and say, "Thank ye, guv'nor," when people gave him sandwiches or coffee or spare change. He looked up, saw me in the window, and waved with his free hand. I waved back, shifted my focus to the water stain on the ceiling for modesty's sake, and pondered what Gemma had told me.

She was sincere. I'd give her that. And underneath the layer of cute she wore like camouflage, there was a toughness to her—a kind of grit—that I liked. Maybe my first impression had been wrong, and she wasn't just some hysterical kid making up fairy tales. Maybe there actually was something to what she'd said. Besides, who was I to argue when there was cash on the table?

At the very least, I could nose around and see what the brother was up to, figure out what the fight between him and his friend had been about, and give Gemma a better story to tell herself about the whole deal. I could help a sad little girl feel like someone cared.

I drank a glass of water at the sink in the corner and pushed back my hair. It was black, kinky-curled, and stuck out from my head every which way. My hair had a mind of its own, and just then it was asking for a fight.

"Wear the *hijab* like *Ummi* did," Reem would say, "and you'll never have to worry about bad hair days."

But headscarves weren't my thing. Never had been. Not even before cancer swallowed my mother whole.

I dialed Gemma's cell.

"It's Scarlett," I said when she picked up. "I'll take the case."

"Thank you." Her voice was small. Relieved. I asked if it was a good time to come over. She said it was and gave me her address. "I really mean it," she whispered. "Thank you."

"Thank me after I've done something, kid," I said, and hung up.

I grabbed my favorite purple tam from the coat hook and put it on. A raincoat would have been nice, too, but all I had was the fly's eye–green umbrella Mook had given me from the Laundromat's lost and found a few months back.

I put the umbrella in my backpack and gave my Goodwill jeans, white T-shirt, and secondhand men's houndstooth coat a once-over. If I smiled nice and behaved, the outfit would do for a visit to the Archers'. I didn't look like a private detective. I didn't look like an orphan. And that was just the way I liked it.

2

Gemma's apartment was in a strip of converted warehouses off Daly Street, on the north end of Las Almas Bay. They were trendy, expensive, and full of people who never took time to look out their own windows and enjoy the view.

By the time I got there, the morning rain had lifted, and people with cloth shopping bags and expensive baby strollers were out and about. Farther south, Daly was nothing but pawnshops, liquor stores, and grimy little joints that would cash your paycheck for half of what it was worth. This far north, it was all organic grocers and coffee shops.

Ten minutes and six nail salons later, I was standing in front of Gemma's building. The place was flat-roofed and long, boring as a nun's underwear, and full of blank-looking picture windows. Gemma was an Archer. The Archers lived on the top floor. I pressed their intercom button, smiled for the camera, and wondered how many freckled, sixteen-year-old brown girls showed up on their video monitor any given day. The door buzzed. I went in and took the freight-sized elevator up.

Gemma opened the door in her goggles and stepped back to let me in. Her movements were quick. Unhappy.

"Hi," she said.

"Your folks home?"

"They're at work. Dad owns Archer Construction. It's a big deal. Mom does interior design."

"What about Oliver?"

She gave me a somber look. "He's here."

"How about an introduction?"

"Come on," she said, and led me down a hall lined with framed black-and-white photos of skyscrapers. The carpet under our feet was thick enough to lose an ankle in. Spotlights lit the pictures like Rembrandts.

"Those are my dad's." She motioned toward the frames. I gave them a closer look.

"He owns all those buildings?" I asked.

"No. He built them."

I was impressed.

We passed an archway leading to a white-walled room with white leather furniture, floor-length white curtains, and white rugs over bleached hardwoods. Lionfish roamed an enormous saltwater aquarium.

"Fish were Dad's hobby last year," Gemma said when she saw me looking. "They were supposed to help him with stress. Now he just pays a guy to clean the tank."

"Maybe he should have tried goldfish first," I said. She shrugged and kept walking until the hall dead-ended at a closed door.

"Ollllivvvverrrr!" She hammered on the wood with a pale fist. There was shuffling behind the door before it opened.

Oliver was easy on the eyes. Handsome, even, in a boy band kind of way. He looked like he worked out, and the zit fairy had only paid a courtesy call instead of an extended visit.

"What?" He scanned me with his blue eyes like a cashier scans frozen peas.

"Oliver, this is my friend Scarlett. I wanted you to meet her."

"Hello, Scarlett. It's a pleasure to make your acquaintance."

He didn't sound like he meant it.

"The pleasure's all mine."

I didn't sound like I meant it, either.

I stuck out my hand, meaning for it to feel like a challenge. Oliver hesitated, his top lip curling into a sneer before he gave in and took hold of my fingers with a grip three notches too tight. As he did, the sleeve of his rugby shirt pulled back, exposing a line of angry red scabs along the inside of his wrist. He noticed that I noticed, jerked his hand back, jammed his fists into his pockets.

"Aren't you a little ... mature to be hanging out with a nine-year-old?" His voice had gone hard.

"It's a Big Sister kind of thing," I said.

He looked at Gemma. Gemma looked worried.

"Funny," he said. "She's hardly underprivileged. And she has a *real* big brother."

"Yet she still came to me...." The sweetness in my voice was anything but.

Oliver scowled. "If you'll excuse me, I've got things to do."

He grabbed the messenger bag leaning against his

bookshelves and pushed past us, slamming the bedroom door as he went. A few seconds later, the front door slammed, too.

Gemma slipped her palm into mine. I wasn't much of a hand-holder, but just then I didn't mind the touch of someone warm and good.

The kid was all right.

Her brother was not.

I never could stand a closed door, and Oliver's was no exception.

"I'm going in," I said.

"So you believe me that something's wrong?" Gemma asked.

"I believe I agreed to take the case," I said, turning the knob.

At first glance, the room was nothing special. Sports posters on the walls. Body spray and locker room funk in the air. It was clean, though. Neat. No clothes piled on the floor, no clutter.

"This isn't normal," Gemma said.

"You mentioned he's not the organized type."

"Yeah. He and Mom used to fight over the mess all the time. He'd say it was his space; she'd say no it wasn't unless he started paying rent. Now that he cleans it, though, she doesn't even come down to this end of the apartment. She thinks she won." Gemma snorted at the last bit.

"Good to know," I said. "Now stay put."

The first thing I did inside the room was walk its perimeter. Next, I memorized the positions of everything I might move or misplace. This had to be a clean sweep. Oliver couldn't know I'd been there.

Once I had the lay of the place, I looked under the bed, mattress, and pillows. Opened desk and bureau drawers all the way to the back. Sifted through anything siftable. Then I hit the closet, reaching between stacks of sweatshirts and sweaters, making sure nothing was hidden behind the perfectly spaced hanging clothes. That's when my hand hit something pinned to a jacket.

"This new?" I held up the small baggie of dried leaves.

"No. He's smoked that stuff since he was thirteen," Gemma said.

I put the baggie back and inspected the rest of the room, right down to fanning the pages of each book on the shelves. Other than Oliver's weed, the place was clean.

It didn't surprise me. Real detective work wasn't anything like what they showed on TV. On TV, clues sat around like giant Easter eggs waiting to be found. In real life, they dressed up like normal things, so that half the time you didn't even know it when they were staring you right in the face.

I wiggled my eyebrows up and down at Gemma to make her smile. She didn't. Then I gave the room another quick once-over and, because I'm a thorough kind of girl, swung the door around to make sure nothing was hiding behind it.

Something was: a clue. And it hadn't bothered to dress up at all.

"This new?" I asked.

Gemma came to my side and pulled the goggles down over her eyes.

"Mom's gonna kill him," she whispered.

Every inch, every single bit of wood on that door, had been carved with different versions of the same interlocking ring design. Some of the rings were ovals, some were shaped like cats' eyes. A few were rectangles with rounded edges. Each had a square at the center with its four corners formed by the overlapping points of the lines.

"Go get a dark crayon and some paper. Quick," I said.

Gemma stared for a few seconds longer and ran out. I studied the door, knowing from the fresh wood smell that the marks hadn't been there long, wondering if maybe the design had something to do with the cuts on Oliver's wrist. A deep, dusty part of my brain told me I'd seen it before. But the kid came back faster than I could clear out the cobwebs and remember where.

"Thanks," I said, tearing the wrapper off her purple crayon. I tucked the shreds into my jeans pocket, flattened a piece of paper over one of the biggest sets of rings, and rubbed the side of the crayon back and forth until the whole image appeared. I did the same thing to a second, more squared-off knot. Then a third. And a fourth. Gemma watched, still as a cat about to pounce. "Let's get out of here," I said when the fifth was done.

As she led me to her room, I put the crayon in my coat, reminding myself to ditch it in a trash can somewhere far away from the Archers' apartment. Maybe I was being too careful, since the chances of Oliver finding a peeled crayon and figuring out it had been used to make rubbings of his artwork were slim to none. But for someone who'd written Gemma off just a few hours earlier as a wound-up kid with an overactive imagination, I was starting to wonder if maybe she was on to something.

"I've got a few more questions," I said once she'd stashed the unused paper in a desk drawer.

"I thought you might." She pushed the goggles onto her forehead and smiled the first real smile I'd seen on her Kewpie doll face.

"I'm going to figure this out, kid," I said, which made her smile even bigger.

Just like I'd hoped it would.

3

I took my time walking back to the bus stop, window-shopping as I went. Four blocks later, I'd managed to pick something up without spending a dime.

I had a tail.

She was tall and blonde and white as marble, with clothes that matched her skin and a face like a cemetery angel. Her tail job wasn't subtle; she slowed when I slowed, stopped when I stopped, and was either lousy at her job or didn't care if I spotted her.

It wasn't the first time I'd been followed. Not by a long shot. Still, I took a second to screw my head on straight. *Get over it and ditch her*, I told myself, and started glancing up and down cross streets for a metro station, wondering what I'd done or who I'd ticked off enough to earn myself a shadow.

I'd gone nearly six blocks when a crowd of men and women spilled out of the building to my left and blocked the sidewalk in front of me. They were damp-headed, glassy-eyed, and moving slow. FYRE, the sign over the door said. HOT YOGA STUDIO.

I shifted toward the curb, brushed up against a parked SUV, noticed the second tail. This one was short. Turquoise streaked through her square-banged black hair. She wore skintight yoga clothes and carried a mat across her back, but she wasn't sluggish or soaked like the yogis leaving the studio. Her getup was all for show.

Shorty moved behind me; Blondie stuck close to the shops. I cleared the crowd, picked up my pace. At the next intersection, I caught sight of a station entrance a hundred yards to my right and crossed fast against the light, metro card in my hand before I hit the turnstiles. I swiped it, went through, looked back. My tails might not have used public transportation enough to have a pass, but they jumped stiles like pros. I kept moving, cutting behind strollers and slow-moving tourists. The pair stayed close, rolling off my picks like WNBA point guards.

The sound of an incoming train rumbled up the stairs to my left. I banked hard, ran down, dove through the mass of people shuffling toward the platform's edge. By the time the train screeched to a stop, I'd put three cars' worth of space between the pale women and me. The train doors opened. I hopped on. Three cars down, so did they. I hugged the pole just inside the door, fighting the crush of bodies as it tried to push me farther inside, ignoring the nasty looks I got for my trouble. The platform cleared. I crouched low and waited for the recorded voice to tell us to stand clear of the closing doors. The voice came. The doors' hydraulics kicked in. I dove for the platform.

All of me made it through. All of my clothes did not.

One corner of my jacket was pinched tight between the sealed doors, and I'd read enough horror stories in the paper to know that these were old, unforgiving trains with safety features that hadn't been state of the art since 1960. I dropped my bag, threw my shoulders back, and slipped the jacket off just in time to watch it disappear into the dark mouth of the tunnel ahead.

My eyes shifted to the car windows gliding past.

21

This was supposed to be the fun part—the part where I got to grin a shit-eating grin and wave a smart-assed wave as my tails rolled helplessly by. Trouble was, they weren't on the train; they were fifteen yards down the platform and closing fast.

Turned out I wasn't so clever after all.

I made for the stairs to my right, trying to forget how much longer Blondie's legs were than mine. In a fair fight, I'd win nine times out of ten. Going two-against-one changed those odds, and not in my favor. So when I spotted a transit cop leaning against the ticket window, I nixed the idea of taking on the pair myself and hoofed it over to him fast.

"Sir, I saw two women back there acting really strange."

I was trying hard to catch my breath. He was trying hard to keep his eyes on my face instead of my chest.

"They went up to this abandoned bag sitting on a bench. It might have just been a yoga mat, but..." I dropped my head lower so he'd realize it wasn't my T-shirt talking. "I heard them say something to each other, and one of them picked it up. I know it's probably nothing, but with all the signs around saying we should report anything suspicious..."

I'd picked the right story. My chest got a lot less interesting.

"Is that them?" He pointed to my tails as they stopped short behind the turnstiles just a few feet away. It was the first head-on look at them I'd had, the first time I'd noticed the rings of pale gold circling the outside edges of their irises. *All the better to see you with, my dear,* I thought, shaking off a shudder and nodding to the cop.

"Stay put," he said.

I gave him my good-girl smile. "Yes, sir."

My tails bolted. The cop took off running. Once he'd cleared the turnstile, I headed up to the street, took a quick look around to make sure I was really alone, and told myself I'd have to do something about my problem with authority.

Later.

I snagged the first taxi I came to and slid down low in the slippery vinyl seat. The rolling lilt of a Hindi radio show filled the cab so that when I gave the driver my address, I couldn't tell if he was nodding at me or agreeing with the announcer. It wasn't until angry honks blared around us and we'd picked up speed that I sat tall, drew a full breath, and considered the particulars of my situation.

Since the Archer case was the only one to come across my desk in the last few weeks, it stood to reason that the women I'd just ditched had gone on the job sometime between Gemma showing up at my office and me leaving her place. That meant Oliver must have called them in, and *that* meant things were getting hot. Fast.

Back in Gemma's room, I'd squeezed her for more info on her family. She'd filled me in on Archer Construction and her mother's interior design business, told me how she and Oliver went to Chandler Academy, a ritzy private school where tuition cost an arm and two legs. I didn't like that she spent a lot of time alone in the apartment with her brother, but the way she told it, he'd all but ignored her for the last month. "He's not home much, and when he is, he mostly stays in his room or Dad's office," she'd said. "He never bugs me anymore."

Still, I'd made her promise to stay out of Oliver's way. "Act normal, don't go in his room, and don't let on that you think anything's wrong," I'd said. It had seemed like enough of a warning at the time. Now I wasn't so sure. I took out my phone and dialed.

"Hello?" Her voice was shaky as an old man on skates.

"It's Scarlett," I said. "What's wrong?"

Nothing came back but the fast breathing of a scared little girl.

"Gemma? Are you okay?"

"Oliver's really mad because I went into his room," she said.

Shit.

I'd screwed up somehow, and now the kid was in trouble.

"It's just Mom again, Oliver," Gemma hollered, her voice loud but blunted, like she'd turned her head away from the phone. "I told her I'm sorry for messing with your stuff."

"Are you safe there, Gemma?" I asked.

"I'm fine, Mom. It's no big deal."

I could hear the lie in her voice. It made me uneasy. *Oliver* made me uneasy. And I was starting to think that the less time Gemma spent around him, the better off she'd be.

"Listen," I said, "is there anyone you could go stay with for a few days?"

"Yes."

"Can you get yourself over there today?"

"I think so."

"Good. Do it, and sooner rather than later. Once you're settled in, send me the address. And don't let Oliver get ahold of your phone. I don't want him figuring out you weren't talking to your mom."

"Sure, Mom. I can do that. But you know, things are so crazy I might not be able to finish my book report this weekend. Maybe I should stay home with Aunt Lucy on Monday so she can help me."

Smart, I thought. Gemma was telling me where she was going and asking if she should avoid being near Oliver at school, all in the same clever breath.

"Go to school," I said, "but only straight there and straight back home to your aunt's. Take everything you'll need for a few days, and stay close to adults you trust."

"All right, Mom. Love you."

"Be careful," I said.

"You too," she answered. And hung up.

Yeah, I thought, keeping my phone in my hand, knowing it was going to stay there until Gemma sent word that she'd gotten to her aunt's. *Me too.*

4

I had the taxi drop me off in a section of brown-stones well south of our apartment so I could walk and clear my head. It was a quiet neighborhood, full of doctors' offices and law firms and white-tablecloth restaurants with bored-looking waiters. The smells coming from kitchen exhaust fans set my stomach singing, but I had a different kind of joint in mind for lunch. The kind where fries came with gravy, and the up-yours ambiance came from the heart.

Half an hour later, I walked through the door of the Rubicon Diner and made straight for my favorite booth. I was lucky it was available; the place was packed.

WE RESERVE THE RIGHT TO REFUSE SERVICE, SO DON'T PISS US OFF. That was what the sign taped to the hostess stand said, and that was what Delilah meant. "My place, my rules," she'd say. "You don't like it, take it up with Decker." The way she figured, one look at all six-foot-muscled-six of her son would end any dispute on the spot. And Delilah almost always figured right.

The diner's walls were plastered with so many photos, sketches, signs, autographed sugar packets, and soup can labels that you could spend hours studying the place and only see half of what was there. As a little girl, I'd loved each and every tacky bit of it. Then, on a cold December day two years earlier, Deck's fingertips had brushed my hand as he reached to refill an empty water glass. He'd mumbled an apology and pulled back fast, but when his eyes lingered on mine like a slow kiss, I'd known it hadn't been an accident. That was the day the decorations turned to faded paper, the moment a boy I'd known all my life had become something...more.

"Afternoon, Scarlett."

Delilah leaned a hip against my table. She was big-bosomed and bowlegged, and wore her scattershot black-and-gray curls pinned carelessly at the top of her head. I'd never seen her in anything but khakis and a T-shirt.

"Hi, Delilah. How about some banana pancakes?"

She arched an eyebrow. "How about you tell me what you've been up to?"

"Aw, come on. I'm starving."

"I only feed kids who stay out of trouble. You staying out of trouble?"

Delilah had been my mother's best friend. She'd promised to keep an eye on me, and it was a job she took to heart.

I slumped against the duct-taped banquette and set my phone close by on the table. "Yeah," I said. "I'm staying out of trouble."

"Yeah or yes?"

"Yes."

Delilah pinched her lips tight.

"I still say it was a mistake letting you graduate early. No kid as smart as you should get cut loose on the streets for two years with nothing better to do than nose around in other people's business. You should have gone straight to college."

In my mind I rolled my eyes. In reality I knew better.

"You know I was bored out of my skull in high school, Delilah. If they hadn't let me test out early, they'd have ended up tossing me instead. Besides, my nosing around in other people's business got the Bus Stop Killer off the streets, didn't it? The cops never would have caught the guy if I hadn't tracked down the kids who saw him grab his last victim."

Delilah sniffed.

"That Detective Morales shouldn't have gotten you involved in the first place. If I were your sister, I'd tell him exactly where to stick that badge of his."

I laughed. "Emmet's a good guy, Delilah."

She leaned in close, one hand on the table.

"Then *he* should be figuring out who murdered your father, not letting you play detective, thinking you're gonna catch the monster yourself."

My throat pinched down tight. She'd hit a nerve best left alone, and it must have shown.

Delilah sagged into her heels. "I shouldn't have said that, hon. I'm sorry."

"How about those pancakes?" I kept my voice steady. It took some doing.

"Gimme a tall stack with monkey chow, Deck," she hollered toward the kitchen. Her voice cut through the room's loud hum of conversation like a dentist's drill. Delilah only cared about etiquette when it wasn't hers.

"Comin' up, Ma!" Decker called back.

Delilah looked at me, lips pursed.

"You drinking coffee?"

"I am."

"You shouldn't."

"So you say, every time I come in."

She waved her hand like I was an especially pesky fly and walked off. I'd get my coffee in the end, but only when Delilah was good and ready.

In the meanwhile, I spread one of the rubbings from Oliver Archer's door out on the table and ran a finger over the design. I knew I'd seen it before, but the harder I tried to think where, the more I couldn't. I was still pondering the thing a few minutes later when Delilah came back.

"Whatcha got there?"

"Some kind of symbol. Do you know it?"

She looked down, drew in a sharp breath, jerked back so fast that coffee sloshed out of the thick brown mug on her tray.

"*Hmm*," I said. "My keen detective skills tell me you do."

"Where did you get that?"

"It's from a case," I said. "Why? You recognize it?"

She looked at me, silent as stone.

"What's the matter, Delilah? Are you gonna tell me about it or not?"

"Whatever you're up to, drop it now." Her voice was barely a whisper. "Get the hell off the streets and ship out to college like you should have done a long time ago."

I wasn't much of a sigher, but for Delilah, I made an exception. "You're wrong about my work, Delilah. It keeps me *out* of trouble. Now what's the deal?"

"No, *you're* wrong, Scarlett. And you're about to run up against the kind of trouble that doesn't give second chances."

"Delilah…"

Her palm shot up, cutting me off. "I can't talk to you right now." She slammed my coffee down, did an about-face, and walked away.

A few minutes later, Decker came out of the kitchen carrying a plate stacked high with pancakes. I tilted the rubbing toward my chest and tried not to notice how tight his shirt was, or how his grin made everything go wobbly from my belly button down. As he wove his way around the restaurant's tight-packed tables, I reminded myself that romances were a lot harder to keep alive than friendships. *Don't hold on,* I thought, *and you'll never have to let go.*

And then he was at my side, grin and all.

"What'd you do to piss Ma off so bad?"

"Damned if I know," I said. "How's school?"

"Same old." He set my pancakes in front of me. "Hasn't been nearly as much fun since you left. Still doing jujitsu?"

"Muay Thai. And yeah, I train when I can."

"Have you told your sister yet?"

"Sure, Deck, I told Reem all about it." There was enough vinegar in my voice to pickle the words. "She said the imam at our mosque would think it's swell that I spend so much time fighting sweaty, half-naked guys and learning Buddhist rituals. Just nifty."

Decker laughed. "Relax. I'm just yanking your chain." He looked around the diner to make sure everyone had food, then wedged himself in across from me. I could feel the heat from his legs through the fabric of my jeans.

"Whatcha got there?" He pointed at my chest.

"If you haven't figured out what *those* are, Deck, it's time you and Delilah had The Talk."

He smiled, not nearly so embarrassed as I wanted him to be. "You know what I mean, smartass."

"Oh . . . the *paper*," I said. "Right."

He waited. I poured syrup on my pancakes and cut off a forkful.

"Show me." He leaned forward, touched my hand to stop me from taking a bite. My heart skipped a beat or three. I handed him the papers.

A muscle twitched in his jaw.

"What is it?" I asked. "I know I've seen it before. I just can't think where."

"Where'd this come from?"

"Like I told Delilah, it's from a case."

He leaned back. Tried to look nonchalant. "You probably saw it in your mosque."

A light flashed on in my brain, but only a dim one. Deck was right; the same design ran through the tile work on our mosque's floor. But that wasn't where I remembered it from. Not really.

"It's in our synagogue, too," he went on. "It's called a Solomon's knot."

"What?"

"You know, King Solomon? The guy who said he'd

divide the baby in half if the two women arguing over it couldn't decide whose it was?"

"Yeah. Sure," I said. "In Islam he's a prophet—peace be upon him. He knew the real mother wouldn't want the baby killed, so he gave it to the one who said she'd rather lose it than let it die."

"Right." Deck nodded. "Well, some people think that since the design's a never-ending link, it symbolizes power—magic, even—and that it's called *Solomon's* knot because the king had magical powers himself."

"And?"

"And people all over the world have used it in their weaving and painting and stuff since forever. Different religions, different cultures—it's everywhere."

"So why'd Delilah go off on me like that?" I said.

He watched me with eyes that tilted down at the corners. That tilt gave him an air of wistfulness—of longing—like he'd lost something only I could find.

"You want more info than that, you'll have to tell me what you've gotten yourself into."

I watched him back. The funny thing was, even though I'd known Deck forever, I'd never really registered the color of his eyes. It's a hard thing to look at a person square, especially when just being near them is enough to knock you ten degrees off-kilter. But I saw them then, saw that each sea-glass-green iris was ringed by the faintest trace of soft, golden flecks.

Goose bumps popped up along my arms. Blondie's and Shorty's hard gold rings had been too distinct to miss. They weren't exactly the same as Deck's, but they were close. *Stick to the case*, I told myself. *Don't let coincidences trip you up.*

"My client's a nine-year-old girl," I said. "I found this symbol carved into the door of her brother's room. He's been acting funny lately. She wants me to figure out why."

"That all you're gonna say?" Decker asked.

"It is."

He rubbed his palm over the stubble on his cheek. Deck never shaved until the afternoon, and on my weaker-willed days I hated him for it. Without saying a word, he pulled the neck of his shirt down, exposing a silver dollar–sized indigo tattoo on the skin of his left pec. Only it wasn't a silver dollar. It was the knot.

"When did you get *that*?" I forced myself to look away.

"Last June."

"Delilah let you?"

"I didn't ask permission."

"I thought nice Jewish boys weren't supposed to get tattoos."

"Who says I'm nice?" He leaned in so close I could feel his breath.

I rolled my eyes and kicked his shin hard enough to make him reach down and rub it. On the way back up, his hand bumped high on the inside of my thigh. He pulled back fast and blushed, but the heat from his fingers lingered on my skin and crept north. Close as we'd been dancing these past two years, there were still some lines we weren't ready to cross. Inner thighs were one.

"Sorry." His guilty little grin was almost enough to sink me. Almost, but not quite.

"Why'd you get the tattoo, Deck?"

He shook his head. "That's not the question you should be asking."

"No? Then what is?"

"*Where*. You should ask me *where* I got it."

I fluttered my lashes. "Okay, Deck. Pretty please with whipped cream and a cherry on top, won't you tell me *where* you got your tattoo?"

"Calamus," he said. "Calamus Tattoos. But you might not be ready yet."

"Ready?"

"Yeah."

My patience hit its limit faster than a college freshman's credit card.

"Care to explain what makes this tattoo place so special? And while you're at it, let me know exactly who put you in charge of deciding what I may or may not be ready for. Because I've got a thing or two to tell them."

My lashes weren't fluttering anymore.

"You aren't going to let this drop, are you?" He shook his head mournfully.

I glared at him.

"Ma's not happy, you know. She's the one who really doesn't think you're ready. I just don't want you to be."

"Ready for what?"

"Remember how, when we were in kindergarten, you lost that tooth on the playground, and I said the tooth fairy would visit you that night?"

"Yeah. I told you there was no tooth fairy and that I'd stay up all night to prove it."

"And you did, right? You stayed up and came in the

next day to tell me you'd caught your mother sneaking money under your pillow."

"I made you cry," I said, feeling guilty for something I'd done a long time ago.

"Yeah. You did. But what if you'd been wrong, Scarlett? Would you have been prepared for that?"

"I didn't have to be. The tooth fairy's not real."

"What if you'd been wrong?"

"You can't be ready for the impossible, Deck."

He shook his head.

"But what if the impossible happened? *That's* what I don't want you ready for, Scarlett. Not yet."

I sighed and put the door rubbings back in my bag.

"You're a piece of work, you know it, Deck?"

"We both are, Scarlett."

He stood up and went back to the kitchen, leaving me to ponder my pancakes. Halfway through the stack, my phone chimed.

Lucy Archer. 2920 East Walker, Apt. 16A.

I really am ok now.

I chased the shot of relief from Gemma with a gulp of cold coffee and texted back.

Stay that way, kid. Be in touch soon.

A few seconds later, a picture popped onto my

screen. It was Gemma, smiling in front of a green awning with THE GODWYN printed across it in all-white caps. The street address she'd given me was underneath that, and the reflection of a doorman with gold epaulets shone in the glass behind her. Funny, but in person I hadn't noticed the pixie tilt of her nose. I saw it now, along with the wide blue innocence in her eyes. She was a sweet kid. A good kid. Life hadn't kicked her in the teeth yet, and even though she was starting to suspect that it might, something in the picture made me want to protect her.

Gemma was still a little girl.

And I'd do whatever I could to help her stay that way.

5

Delilah wouldn't come near me, not even to bring the check. I left a ten on the table, headed to my office over the Laundromat, and looked up the address for Calamus Tattoos. It was at the corner of Third and Doyle, a part of town nice folks had given up on years ago. Next, I searched the city's online public records database to see who owned the place. RECORD NOT FOUND was all that came back, which meant someone had lost the information, by accident or on purpose. Either way, it was a dead end.

The afternoon was getting old fast, and it crossed my mind that waiting until morning to visit Calamus might be smart. But patience had never been one of my virtues, and smart only got you so far. So I grabbed my blackjack and headed out.

The blackjack was smooth and solid, just under a foot of polished wood that started narrow at one end and widened all the way to an inch and a quarter at the other. A stiff leather strap looped through the narrow part and fit around my wrist just fine. I'd found the thing in a junk-shop bin full of splintered wooden spoons and figured it must have belonged to a beat cop back at the turn of the century. It wasn't as threatening as a knife or intimidating as a gun, but I was fast, knew where to aim, and could use it to knock a grown man out cold with one good whack.

Downstairs, Mook was in his usual spot on the stoop, smoking one of the black tobacco cigarettes he bought by the case from a guy who smuggled them in from Spain. All cigarette smoke turned my stomach, but these were a special kind of awful, like dead skunks in hot tar.

Mook had lived in the first-floor apartment behind the Laundromat for as long as I could remember. He was tall and wiry, with long black hair pulled into a ponytail at the nape of his neck. He wore his black jeans, white tank top, and black leather duster like a uniform, never sweating in summer, never buttoning the duster in winter.

"Where are you headed, *akht*? Haven't you had enough excitement for one day?" His dark eyes scanned the street as he spoke. *Akht* meant "little sister" in Arabic. He called himself my *mu'aqqibat*—my guardian angel. Mook was full of shit.

"Out," I said. "I'm on the clock."

"Be that as it may, you haven't answered my question."

"Gimme a break, Mook. I'm in a hurry."

He swung his head toward me and hooked the cigarette between two long fingers. Mook reminded me of a raven, all scary-beautiful and hollow-boned.

"You wouldn't be thinking of going to one of the less savory neighborhoods in our fair city, would you, my dear?"

"Why would I do something like that?" I said. "I'm working for a private school kid from over on North Daly."

He took a drag and let the smoke hover around his half-closed eyelids.

"One of the conditions of our arrangement, *akht*, is

that you check in with me on a regular basis. You gave your word to your sister. Break it, and I'll help her find a women's college out in the middle of nowhere willing to give a smart girl like you a scholarship."

Tantrums weren't my thing. Drama, either. Still, Mook knew how to get under my skin like a bad case of splinters. How could he always tell when I was doing something I shouldn't?

"I'll be home before dark," I said. "Don't worry."

"I never do."

"Great. Can I go now?"

He took another languid drag and blew it out.

"We've chatted about respect before, haven't we, *akht*? About how those who want it must show it first?"

The immediate response that came to mind was about as respectful as a pop in the nose. I kept my lips zipped.

One side of Mook's mouth lifted into a smile. "Did that hurt?"

"Did what hurt?"

"Not saying whatever it was you wanted to?"

"Like you don't even know."

The smile spread to both sides of his face. He pulled another cigarette out and lit it from the stub of the old one.

"Those'll kill you," I said. My bus was rounding the corner.

"Go," he said.

And for once, I listened.

As it turned out, the corner of Third and Doyle wasn't just rough, it was flat-out scary. Even the bus driver must have thought so, because when I pulled the signal cord to get off, he asked what address I wanted, drove past the stop, and dropped me smack in front of Calamus Tattoos.

This part of Las Almas looked like it had been on the losing side of a war. Buildings sagged on crumbling foundations. Cardboard, tape, and rags marked the broken windows of apartments where people actually lived. The loose ends of those rags flapped in the late afternoon breeze like flags of surrender.

Except for a lone figure half a block over, wrapped head to toe in dirty fabric and swaying back and forth on its feet, the only sign of life I could find was a mangy street mutt watching me with the one eye left in its head. Dogs set me on edge, and this one was no exception. I watched, making sure it wasn't sizing me up for dinner. It didn't move. I slipped my blackjack from my bag just in case and went up the stairs.

Calamus didn't look like a tattoo shop at all. There were no neon signs, no painted windows to lure in drunks and bored housewives. In fact, the place was a church. Sure, it was smaller than most and had no visible stained glass windows, but there was no mistaking the central arch, broad columns, and rectangular towers flanking its main facade like sentries. The whole thing was built from blocks of granite dulled down to an ugly shade of crud by years of accumulated car exhaust and city grime.

I climbed thirteen stone steps and stood in front of big, arched double doors. They were wooden and looked half a foot thick, with heavy bands of metal stretching from the inset hinge, all the way across to the opposite side. At the center of the right-hand door was a small sign with CALAMUS TATTOOS written in swirling script alongside the etched image of a quill.

I weighed my options. Technically this was a kind of store, so walking in should be fine. And you didn't have to knock before you went into a church, either. But the whole situation felt odd as rubber socks. Good manners weren't usually a concern of mine, but something kept me from barging into the place. Made me give a knock too timid for even church mice to hear. I tried again with the tip of the blackjack, but even then the door's thick wood swallowed the sound. Short of beating on the thing like a fool, it was the best I could do. I rocked back on my heels. Looked up. Rocked back a little further.

Letters, airy and looping, were carved into the dirty stone over the doorway. WE REMAIN UNVANQUISHED, they spelled out. In Syriac.

Not that I was fluent in ancient Aramaic languages; I was a modern language kind of girl. But those particular words were engraved across the one thing of our father's that my sister and I had left: a bottle forged of heavy, time-blackened metal, with a broad bottom, narrow top, and a thick lid I'd never managed to pry off.

A lid, I suddenly remembered, that was stamped with a deep impression of Solomon's knot.

I thought about banging my head against the church's granite, but since the dog and the swaying weirdo were still nearby, I settled for a quiet sigh of frustration. *That* was why I'd recognized the design from

Oliver's door. *That* was why Deck's line about mosque floor tiles hadn't rung true. Solomon's knot had been right in front of me my whole life, on an Egyptian relic handed down through my father's family for centuries. Only I'd never bothered to notice it. To *really* notice it.

I knew the bottle was valuable, though. *Abbi* told us once that it was worth more than we could imagine, but that selling it would be the same as selling our past and future all at once. "Money can't buy history," he'd said. "Or peace."

That was why, not long before he died, *Abbi* had hidden the real bottle in a safe deposit box and left two antique copies of it out in the open for the whole world to see—one in our living room curio cabinet, one on the crowded back office desk in his bookstore. The office copy had been stolen the night he was murdered. The other was right where he'd left it.

After *Ummi* died, Reem and I found the safe deposit key tucked inside the folded fabric of her best *hijab*. Tracking down which bank it belonged to had been my first successful detective gig. I'd taken the bottle home and tried to convince Reem we should sell it. As far as I was concerned, money would have made our lives a whole lot easier, and the only difference between the real bottle and the fake we still had was a pair of hash marks cut into the original's base.

Reem saw things differently. She dragged me to the bank, put the bottle back in the safe deposit box, and told me she'd kick my ass four ways to Sunday if I ever messed with it again.

A passing metro train shook the sidewalk grate behind me. I looked away from the doorway inscription and scoped out the street again. The swaying gray man and the dog had stayed put. The sun was dropping fast. A car backfired in the distance.

With my hand on the wrought-iron door handle, I told myself it must have been my *Qadar* that brought me to this place. My fate. Maybe I'd get lucky and find some answers inside. Then again, maybe I wouldn't. After all, luck had never been my friend, and *Qadar* was a tricky thing.

Insha'Allah, I whispered, pulling open the door. *If God wills it.*

6

A dim floor lamp cast shadows in the waiting area of Calamus Tattoos. It was a small space, partitioned off from the church sanctuary by a cascade of chipped wooden beads that hung in an arched doorway. Chairs covered in faded silk cushions lined the wall. A coffee table with curling legs and an inlaid top stood in front of one of the couches, stacked with ashtrays and old copies of *Inked* magazine. There was no rack of pre-drawn tattoo designs for customers to flip through, no cash register. Other than a few faded travel posters with pictures of sand dunes and Arabic writing, the walls were bare as toy store shelves the day after Christmas.

"Hello?" I said. "Anybody here?"

Footsteps answered.

The man who came through the beads was somewhere between short and tall, with skin the color of weak tea. Wavy silver hair fell loose from his widow's peak to his shoulders. His mustache and goatee were just so, his faded jeans, leather vest, and long-sleeved black T-shirt hung easy from his lean frame. The faded logo of a thrash metal band peeked out between the buttons of the vest.

"*As-salaamu alaikum*," he said. "Peace be upon you." He gave me a once-over and crossed his arms in front of his chest. "You're too young for a tattoo."

"*Wa alaikum as-salaam*," I answered. "I don't want a tattoo."

He stared at me with uncomfortably intelligent eyes. They were brown. And gold-free.

"My name's Scarlett," I said. "I'm trying to help a friend."

It was my standard introduction, since telling adults I was a private detective usually made them treat me like a toddler playing dress-up.

He kept staring.

"This is an interesting place," I said. "You the owner?"

51

He tilted his head. It wasn't much of an answer. I reached into my bag and took out one of the rubbings.

"Could you tell me about this design? A friend of mine from the East Side has it tattooed over his heart. He said he got it done here."

I held up the paper and waited, ready to be just as quiet as the old man, and for just as long. Thirty seconds clicked by, feeling like a thousand.

"It's just a design I do," he finally said. "Nothing special. And as I told you, you'd be too young for me to ink even if it wasn't *haraam*." His deep voice seemed to come from the earth under his feet. Each consonant bounced off the top of his palate, each vowel echoed.

"I know tattoos are forbidden for Muslims," I said, "but as I told *you*, that's not why I'm here."

He smiled faintly.

"Anyway," I said, "I don't think this *is* just a design. I think there's a lot more to it than that."

The smile disappeared. "If this knot is so important to your friend, why doesn't he come ask me about it himself?"

"Because *she's* only nine."

He lifted his hand and smoothed his goatee, pondering. Exactly what, I couldn't say, but the whole process ended with a blink and a wave of his hand. "As I've pointed out, my dear," he said, "you yourself are not of an age to be in this establishment. I suggest you leave now if you want to catch the next bus. Good day."

He turned and walked out. Beads clacked in his wake. I gave the waiting area one last look and made peace with the fact that my bus fare across town hadn't bought me any new info about Solomon's knot.

Buck up, buttercup, I told myself. Because new questions could be better than old answers, and I'd just gotten plenty. Like why a Middle Eastern, sharia law–spouting grampa would hang out in a tattoo parlor church. And how the hell he'd known I was a Muslim in the first place.

The street outside Calamus was empty except for the rag guy. The dog was gone. There were no tails or bogeymen waiting for me in the fading evening light. I tucked a clump of curls back into my tam, took my blackjack out of my bag, and slid it up my right sleeve. Its smooth wood was cold comfort against my skin.

The bus stop was a block past the rag man, and on the

same side of the street. If I crossed the road, he'd know I was trying to avoid him, and I'd just have to cross back anyway. Besides, I knew how to defend myself. *Don't move, creep*, I thought. *Don't freakin' move.*

I started toward him at a steady clip. The figure's sway didn't change. As the distance between us shrank, I could make out a long, dingy scarf wrapped around his neck and up over his nose. A brimmed hat with earflaps covered his brow. His gloves were filthy. Not an inch of flesh was visible. My hand tightened around the blackjack.

At first, the sound coming out of him was so quiet I assumed he was telling himself a tale. But the closer I got, the more it took on a musical drone. The rag man was singing.

Little fingers of caution skittered up my spine.

I kept walking.

The sound changed.

"Stay away," he hissed, dragging his *S* through the rest of the phrase like a dying man's last breath. "Stay away...."

I gave the blackjack another squeeze, kept my feet moving, and didn't stop until I'd reached the broken-down bus kiosk.

From the corner of my eye, I could see the rag man, still swaying. I knew he wasn't going to come after me, knew it in my bones. Still, it wasn't until I heard the whine of a bus engine that my grip on the blackjack loosened and my heart eased down out of my throat.

"Gettin' dark," the fleshy driver said when I climbed aboard. She glanced up into her rearview mirror at the empty bus. "Glad to have your company."

"Amen to that," I said, and settled into the seat behind her.

7

The General was curled up under an old mover's blanket in the alley next to my building, squinting at a tattered copy of the *Las Almas Globe*.

"Whatcha reading, General?" I asked.

"Stories," he said with a toothless grin. "Nothin' but stories."

I fished a five out of my pocket and gave it to him. He rubbed the bill between his fingers and sniffed it. I didn't ask why.

"You're a peach, m'dear," he said, squirreling the money away under his shirt. "A right peach." I told him good night. He was already back to his newspaper, too distracted to reply.

Inside, our apartment was pitch black and cold as a coffin. Reem had graduated from med school two years earlier and was doing her residency at the roughest hospital in Las Almas. I didn't see much of my sister. I missed her.

I flipped on the overhead light, slipped off my shoes before I stepped through the door, and carried my bag of groceries to the kitchen. It was as basic as they come: refrigerator, stove, sink, table, chairs. There was a toaster, too, along with an old-fashioned coffee percolator and an antique boom box that played cassettes. Ugly brown flowers crisscrossed the yellow wallpaper. I noticed a corner of it peeling up, so I put the groceries away, took a little tube of glue from the cabinet by the sink, and tacked the corner down. Then I slogged back to the living room, grabbed *Abbi*'s fake bottle from the curio cabinet, and flopped onto the couch.

Things were getting intense, and it had me thrown. For the most part, detective work was boring. Uncomplicated. I tracked down lost and stolen things, found people who didn't want to be found, and figured out who was cheating on whom.

Gemma Archer's case was different.

For one thing, Blondie and Shorty had started tailing me just an hour or so after I'd met Oliver. For another, there was the knot—the one Oliver had a bad case of the obsessions over, the one inked onto Decker's perfect chest, the one stamped into the lids of *Abbi*'s bottles. It was enough to convince me Gemma was probably right about Quinn Johnson's death not being a simple case of teenage angst run amok.

I ran my finger over the words etched into the bottle and tried to pull its lid off for the millionth time. No dice.

The bottle itself was small and dense and cool in my hand, an exact replica of the priceless one *Abbi* had tucked away in the safe deposit box. I traced the Syriac letters etched into it, wondered how a visit from a scared little girl could have stirred up so much so fast. The whole thing gave me an aspirin-proof headache that wasn't going to go anywhere unless I made some progress on the case.

Problem was, there were too many angles to cover all at once. I set the bottle on the glass-topped coffee table. Got up. Paced. When that didn't help, I went to the kitchen and played one of the plastic cassettes of Arabic music that *Ummi* had loved so much. Our imam here in Las Almas said music was *haraam*, but *Ummi* came from a long line of Sudanese Muslim musicians with songs in their blood.

I thought of her standing in front of her creaky old blue-and-white ironing board, head bouncing to the music's nasal singing and tambourine beat as she forced wrinkles out of everything from headscarves to socks. She always took off her *hijab* before she worked, letting her long, graying curls hang down her back. Unlike mine, her curls were smooth and beautiful. *Abbi* would always touch them as he walked past, smiling a smile meant only for her.

And I pictured *Abbi*, sitting at the table, reading aloud to us from his beloved old copy of *One Thousand and One Nights*. My favorite story was about Sheherazade, how she kept her husband, King Shahryar, from beheading her on their wedding night and for a thousand nights after that by telling tales so wonderful he couldn't bear not knowing how they ended. Outside of *Ummi*, Reem, and me, stories had been the only thing that brought my *abbi* joy.

I closed my eyes and pressed against them with the heels of my hands. Heard *Abbi*'s warm voice bringing jinn, princes, magic fish, and monkeys to life. "Sheherazade refused to let anyone write her story for her," he'd told me one cold Sunday morning as *Ummi*'s steam iron hissed. "And you must do the same."

Then I heard the General's voice in my head. *Stories...Nothin' but stories.*

"Maybe," I whispered to the dark. "But stories get told for a reason."

I grabbed my laptop from the counter and sat down at the kitchen table.

"Talk to me," I said as the *Globe*'s front page loaded. "Tell me something new."

❈

That day's paper had nothing good to say. The city of Las Almas was broke. Fifty police officers and firefighters had been laid off. A tsunami had washed a small island country out to sea. So I pulled up the archived story about Quinn Johnson's suicide, and this time I didn't skim.

Local Teen's Death Ruled a Suicide

LAS ALMAS—According to witnesses, fifteen-year-old Quinlan Johnson jumped to his death from the Baker Street Bridge late

Friday afternoon. Construction barriers for ongoing renovations blocked motorists' view of the situation as it unfolded, but pedestrians on the walkway witnessed the tragedy. Jogger Robert Goncalves saw Johnson sitting on the external guardrail, throwing what appeared to be scraps of paper into the water. "I tried to get to him," Goncalves said in a statement to the media. "I just wasn't fast enough."

According to Goncalves, an unidentified woman reached Johnson before he fell. "He told her something I couldn't hear," Goncalves said. "Right after that, she grabbed his arm, and then he jumped. She couldn't hold on."

Police declined to identify the unnamed witness.

Quinlan Johnson was the son of Archer Construction senior vice president Bradford Johnson and cardiologist Caroline Whittaker-Johnson. He is survived by his parents and an eleven-year-old brother, Samuel.

I reread the last paragraph. Twice.

Quinn's father worked for Archer Construction. Oliver's father, Arthur, had founded Archer Construction. It wasn't much, but it was a loose thread worth tugging. I plugged the company's name into the newspaper's search window. So many articles came up I had to jump back eight screens to get to the first, about a young business with a spanking-new contract to renovate an old hotel lobby. From there the articles ran longer, the projects grew, and the price tags got downright obscene. There were business profiles of Gemma's dad, society shots of her mom all dolled up and smiling at charity galas. Small building projects gave way to big ones. Then came stadiums. Skyscrapers. The newer the article, the more massive the project. And everything seemed to run smooth as fresh-shaved legs, right up until Fagin Inc. hired Archer Construction to build The Parker.

The Parker was going to be the biggest thing the world had ever seen—taller than the Burj Khalifa in Dubai, sleeker than the Shanghai World Financial Center, greener than 30 St Mary Axe in London. It would house offices leased on the cheap to charities and not-for-profits, a mall full of fair trade stores run by at-risk teens, and subsidized apartments for families with foster kids. The whole thing sounded too good to be true. And maybe it was.

From the beginning, work on The Parker had been held up by permit battles, labor disputes, hijacked supply shipments, and equipment sabotage. Vandals broke into Archer's on-site trailer four different times. The mayor himself was overheard telling his assistant the whole thing was jinxed. Still, one of the last articles posted before Quinn Johnson's death included a quote, issued through lawyers, by Fagin Inc.'s "elusive and as-yet-unphotographed" founder, George Fagin. "The Parker is the very embodiment of our company's commitment to fostering dignity, independence, and economic security for all," he'd said. "Nothing will prevent its completion."

A sketch under the quote showed what the finished building would look like. I clicked it into full screen, took a sharp breath when I realized what I was looking at.

Two towers spiraled up like Jack's own beanstalks, united at the base by twenty glassed-in floors. Above that, they rose, separate but side by side, to a series of interwoven skybridges near the top. The skybridges hovered in space, twisting into an infinite, impossible version of Solomon's knot that linked the towers just before they touched the clouds.

Ummi's cassette ran out. Clicked off.

The apartment went quiet.

And then a knock loud as gunfire came from the front door, sending me nearly out of my skin.

I gave the picture one last look and went to the door. *Ummi* had painted over its peephole long ago, after the cancer metastasized to her brain and made her paranoid about people in the hall looking in. Reem and I hadn't had the heart to scrape it off.

"Who is it?" I said.

"Ees Meester Prazsky. Your seester say commode not flush right. I come to feex."

I undid the two chain locks and threw the dead bolt. Our super, Mr. Prazsky, was as hard to pin down as a soft-boiled egg, and when he came to your door, you didn't let him get away. Not even if you were in the middle of busting a hole the size of Cincinnati in your case.

"You're working late tonight, aren't you, Mr. P?" I said as the door swung open.

"Indeed," came the voice. Only this time there was no accent. And no Mr. Prazsky, either.

8

I slammed all my weight against the door. It stopped short of the latch and flew open, sending me sprawling onto the floor. Air shot out of my lungs. Pain streaked through my left wrist. By the time I got to my feet, the stranger was in our apartment, door closed behind him.

He was tall, with dark hair, broad shoulders, and knife-edge cheekbones. In less dire circumstances, I might have called him handsome. As it was, I called him a threat.

"*As-salaamu alaikum,*" he said.

There was no way in hell I was going to wish him peace in return.

"I don't know who you are," I said, "but I want you gone."

"I'm sorry." He didn't sound sorry at all. "I would not have had you fall. For that, I apologize."

He moved closer. I moved back.

"What did you do to Mr. Prazsky?" I said.

"Not a thing. Though we did have a brief conversation about an empty apartment on the seventh floor. Fascinating people, Ukrainians. Lovely accents."

"Look," I said, working hard to sound pissed off instead of scared. "I've had a long day. Tell me what you want so we can wrap this up fast."

He looked unimpressed.

"My name is Asim," he said. "I work with Manny."

"Manny?"

"The gentleman you just visited."

"The tattoo guy?"

"The tattoo guy."

"Well." I leaned against the arm of the love seat behind me and hugged my throbbing wrist to my chest. "Ain't that a helluva thing."

"May I sit?" Asim asked.

"No."

That earned me the kind of scowl a man can only pull off if he's used to being obeyed.

"Look," I said, "judging by your greeting, you're Muslim, right?"

He nodded. Barely.

"Then you know I can't be alone with you. You're a man. We're not related. It's *haraam*."

He smiled. Not cruelly, not dangerously, but with a grim intensity that didn't sit right.

"From what I've seen," he said, "you have very little regard for either your faith or your obligations as a proper young Muslim woman."

He had me dead to rights on that one. I only wished I knew exactly what he'd seen—and how.

"Tell me why you're here," I said. "Or did you want to play twenty questions instead?"

He studied me like a little boy deciding whether or not to pull the legs off a spider.

"I'm here to extend an invitation," Asim said. "Manny requests the pleasure of your company on Monday afternoon at Calamus. One o'clock."

"I was just there," I said. "He didn't seem too keen on conversation."

"You found us sooner than we expected. Manny wasn't ready."

"Expected?"

"Yes."

"Why the hell would he be *expecting* me?"

Asim stared at me with the same disapproving look I got from grumpy old-timers at the mosque.

"You are disrespectful and profane," he said. "Even so, there is much of your father in you."

That knocked me back a few pegs.

"You knew *Abbi*?"

"You can discuss that on Monday. With Manny."

"No," I said, getting all kinds of angry. "You're going to tell me what you know about my father. Now."

He ignored me and looked around the room. Patronizing people sucked. Dismissive people were worse.

I stood up. "Tell. Me. What. You. Know."

His eyes settled on the bottle replica I'd left on the coffee table.

"Don't touch it." I tensed like a missile ready to launch.

A smile flickered across his lips. He picked the bottle up, turned it over and around in his hand.

"We remain unvanquished," he said softly.

"Put it down!"

He turned toward me in a kind of daze, like he'd forgotten I was there.

"The *Shubaak* must be safeguarded," he said. "I'm taking it with me."

"The hell you are!" I charged him. He blocked me with one hand, lifted the bottle beyond my reach with the other.

"You're a bully!" I shouted. "And a thief!"

He bent his head toward me, so close I couldn't help looking into his eyes. The gold rings I saw there were a sucker punch to the gut.

"I am a warrior."

He went to the door.

"Monday. One o'clock."

The door clicked closed.

I collapsed onto the couch, and let the dead bolt be.

Decker answered on the first ring.

"Hey." He sounded relieved and worried all at once.

"Tell me what's going on, Deck."

I was numb. Hollowed out by fear. Shaky from the slow tide of adrenaline leaving my veins.

"Deck?"

"Did you go to Calamus?" he asked.

"Yes."

"And?"

"And nothing." I sank back into the couch cushions. My wrist throbbed. My mouth was dry. My eyes were on the door Asim had closed ten minutes earlier.

"I shouldn't have let you go alone." His words tumbled out all at once. "I should have taken you myself. It's just…"

"Let me?" I said, grateful for the sudden prickle of anger. "Since when do you *let* me do anything?"

Silence.

"Tell me what's happening, Deck."

"Nothing. I'm concerned about you is all."

I rubbed the bridge of my nose with my good hand. Told him he was lying.

The tension on the line was thick enough to chew.

"Why won't you talk to me, Deck?"

"They won't…" He hesitated.

"They?"

He cleared his throat. "Listen, Scarlett, can I come over?"

I wanted him there, wanted to press my back against his chest, feel his arms wrap around me tight enough to make the world go away.

I made my voice harsh to hide the longing behind it.

"Can you explain why someone named Asim just broke into our apartment and walked off with one of the only things Reem and I had left to remind us of *Abbi*?"

"I...I need to see you, Scarlett." His voice broke in the middle of my name.

"Stay home, Deck. It's late."

I reached into my jeans pocket, took out the scraps of crayon wrapper from Gemma's apartment.

"You know I'd tell you everything if I could," he said.

"You would?"

"Yeah," he said softly. "I would. You're important to me, Scarlett."

"I know."

"Good."

I let the strips of paper flutter to the coffee table.

"Call me tomorrow, okay?" he said.

"Maybe."

I hung up before he could say anything else. Pictured his face. And tried to forget how much the gold rings in Asim's eyes reminded me of the ones in his.

9

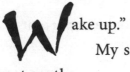ake up."

My sister was shaking my shoulder, and not gently.

I opened one eye. According to the clock on my bedside table, it was quarter to six. AM. I'd dropped off sometime after two.

"Please let me sleep, Reem," I mumbled, rolling toward the wall.

She jabbed my ribs. "Wash up."

There was no getting out of it. Last Friday, I hadn't gone to mosque for *Jumu'ah*, the main group prayer of the week. And even though Muslim women didn't technically have to go, it made Reem about as happy as a cat in a kennel when I skipped. "I can't force you to believe what you don't, Lettie," she'd told me once. "But you have to commit to *something*, even if it's only showing up for *Jumu'ah*."

Now it was just before sunrise, and she wanted me up for the first of the day's five prayers. Plus, she'd made sure I had enough time to perform *wudu*, the ritual cleansing every good little Muslim kid learns to do before they unroll their prayer rug. Considering how much she let me get away with in general, it really wasn't a lot to ask. But that didn't make getting out of bed any easier.

The wrist I'd hurt the night before was as big as a baseball, so I threw on an oversize sweatshirt and let the sleeves hang low. As for *Abbi*'s missing bottle, there was no hiding the fact that it was gone. I'd just have to hope Reem wouldn't notice. Skirting the truth with my sister was one thing; outright lies were another. If she asked, I'd have to tell her about Asim. God knows, part of me wanted to anyway.

I washed, prayed, folded up my rug, and tried to crawl back into bed.

Reem caught me by the arm. "No way. I've got an hour before work, and we're going to spend it together."

"Come on," I said. "I barely slept last night."

"Join the club, Lettie. Now move it."

Reem was short and tough, and had the muscled legs and hard head of a soccer player. She was the strongest person I knew. The prettiest, too, though most people never bothered looking past her *hijab* to notice. The day after our mother died, Reem put on one of her head-scarves and hadn't gone out uncovered since. Before that, my sister had worn her hair loose and her jeans tight. Now that she was covered, only the skin of her hands and face showed.

"Where were you Friday?" she asked.

"Rescuing a kitten from a tree."

That bought me a look, and not a nice one.

"Working, okay? I was working." I sat down at the kitchen table. Reem cracked eggs into a bowl. There was a bag of my favorite croissants in front of me. She must have picked them up on her break the day before.

"Hunting *Abbi*'s killer again?"

I shrugged. "Maybe."

"Dad died seven years ago, Lettie."

"And they still haven't caught the guy who did it," I shot back. "Doesn't it bother you that *Abbi*'s killer is out there right now, laughing at the police? At us?"

"'Hold to forgiveness, command what is right, and turn away from the Ignorant,'" Reem said. "Like the Quran tells us."

"Whatever." I got up and tossed the croissants into the oven. Reem sighed and broke up the yolks with a fork.

"I think it's time we found you a college, Lettie," she said. "It was the right thing to do, letting you finish high school early. But you've got too much time on your hands now, and that's no good for anyone in a town like Las Almas."

"We can't afford college," I said.

"No, not if we have to pay. But you're smart. Plenty of places would give you a scholarship. Or we could take out another loan."

"We have to pay off med school first."

"You're stalling," she said.

"Yeah. I am. But we agreed I'd stay here until you finished your residency."

"I know." Reem shook her head and pushed her hair behind her ear with the back of her hand.

"Anyway," I said, ready to change the subject. "I'm on a new case. A little girl wants me to figure out why her brother's acting funny. She's worried about him."

Reem smiled and poured the eggs into the pan. "Sounds harmless enough. Think you can help her?"

My sister was a sucker for sob stories.

"I'm going to try."

She nodded. Gave me a sly sideways glance. "And do you have any idea why Delilah was so worked up when she called me yesterday?"

Maybe Reem wasn't such a sucker after all.

"Delilah called?" I tried to sound innocent.

"Right after you left the Rubicon. She said she was worried about you, that you'd taken a case she thought was too dangerous. When I pressed her for details, she said it was just a feeling she had. She thinks your obsession with *Abbi*'s murder has started to cloud your judgment."

"Delilah's a worrier," I said. "You know that."

Reem frowned at the eggs. "I do, but I agree with her that you've got to find a way to make peace with *Abbi*'s death. You have to let go."

"Like you let go of *Ummi*'s?" I said. "Trying to save every person who walks through those emergency room doors?"

Reem stiffened. "That's not fair."

She was right. So was I.

"Losing *Abbi* and *Ummi* wasn't fair," I said. "Forcing ourselves to accept their deaths and move on wouldn't be fair, either. We're both dealing with things the best we can. I respect your choices. You need to do the same for mine."

She turned off the burner. "Get plates," she said.

The bunched-up muscles in my shoulders relaxed. If Reem was willing to back off, so was I. Besides, the kitchen was warm, the sky was getting lighter outside, and it was hard to stay tense with a percolator gurgling in the corner.

I took down two plates and pulled the croissants from the oven. Reem brought over the eggs. "*Bismillah*," we said over our food. Then we ate.

It would have bothered our mother if she'd known how rare a thing it was for Reem and me to sit down together for meals. *Ummi* always made sure the three of us were at the table for breakfast and dinner. And for a while after her death, Reem and I had kept up the tradition as best we could. Reem was only twenty then, finishing college and trying to raise me and mourn our mother all at the same time. But once she got into med school and her clinical rotations started, we were lucky if we saw each other more than a few minutes a day. It got worse during her internship. And now that she'd started her residency, I barely saw her at all.

"Tell me more about your case." Reem spooned jam onto her croissant.

I told myself to stick to the basics. Just the bare bones.

"I don't know much yet. Supposedly the brother started going out a lot with new friends, spending all his time on the streets. His sister thinks he got mixed up with some bad stuff."

"That can happen when kids are left on their own too much." Reem smiled at me with her clear, honest eyes.

I didn't respond. I didn't have to.

"You think you're so hard, Lettie," she said with a sigh. "But you haven't seen the kinds of things people do to each other, to themselves...."

She stopped talking and rubbed at a spot on the table that wasn't there.

"Tell me about work," I said, realizing only after the words had come out that I wasn't really changing the subject at all.

Rueful. That was the word for the look she gave me.

"Gunshot wounds," she said. "Overdoses. Heart attacks. The usual."

She stopped talking and pushed bits of egg around her plate.

My sister looked as wrung out as an old dishrag. Still, I knew she needed to be at the hospital, doing her heart's work. *Ummi* had put off going to the doctor when she lost weight for no reason, had kept quiet through weakness and fatigue because she hadn't wanted to wear a skimpy hospital gown. There were no laws in Islam forbidding women from going to the doctor when they needed to, even when only a man or a non-Muslim was available. She could have gotten help right away. Should have. But a lifetime of worrying about modesty and rules and putting other people's needs ahead of her own made her keep the illness secret. It wasn't until she'd started wandering away and getting lost, weeping for no reason and babbling about jinn and ancient curses, that Reem had dragged her to the hospital. By then the cancer had spread too far to stop. The *ummi* we knew was gone even before her body died three months later.

That was when Reem decided to become a doctor. She wanted to start a clinic of her own where traditional women like *Ummi* would feel comfortable going before they were too sick to help. But it was hard, the work she did. Hard on her mind and body, hard on her soul.

"Hey," I said gently. "Do you know what happened to *Abbi's* old copy of *One Thousand and One Nights*?"

She took a deep swallow of coffee, grateful not to have to talk about work anymore.

"Why?"

"I was just thinking about it last night," I said. "Remembering *Abbi* sitting here, reading to us from it. I miss those stories."

She put her cup down and picked at the cuticle on her thumb.

"I miss *him*," she said.

"Yeah."

She started to stand up. "It's in the drawer of my bedside table. I'll get it for you."

I put my hand on her shoulder. "Sit. Have another cup of coffee."

Reem smiled. She had no idea how beautiful she was.

"Remember the rest of your prayers today," she said. "All of them. And you need to run some laundry."

"Sure," I said, meaning that sure, I'd do the laundry. I wasn't going to have time to pray four more times, but Reem didn't need to add that to her list of worries.

"Anything else on your schedule?" she asked.

"Nope."

She didn't buy it.

"Tell Mook where you're going, Lettie."

"Okay."

"Let Emmet worry about tracking down *Abbi*'s killer. He cares about you—about us. And he promised *Ummi* he'd keep looking, even after the case went cold."

"I will."

"I mean it."

"I know."

"And, Scarlett?"

"Yeah, Reem?"

"Be good."

"Always."

Just before nine o'clock, I was outside my office door, spilling hot chocolate with one hand and trying to fit my key into the lock with the other.

"It's open," a voice called from inside.

I turned the knob, and there was Oliver Archer, in my chair with his feet on my desk, spinning a phone against the palm of his hand.

"Good morning," he said.

I sized him up again, from his shaggy brown hair to his gray Chuck Taylors. There was a mean kind of emptiness to him, like he'd left his soul hanging in his closet that morning. But he was soft, too. Spoiled. I could drop him faster than a bad boyfriend.

"I'd have been here to let you in if only you'd called," I said with a smile. "Then again, locks don't seem to be a problem for you, do they?"

He leered at me. "I didn't want to ruin the surprise. Besides, Gemma made it so easy to find you, what with leaving your business card in her sock drawer and all."

Damn. The cards.

I'd had a thousand printed up a few months ago and scattered stacks of them across school bathrooms all over town, Chandler Academy's included. Gemma must have found one and decided I was worth a try. Business was always appreciated. Visits from clients' psychotic brothers were not.

At least the cards only showed my first name, cell number, and office address. Reem had gotten rid of our landline a long time ago, and I never told clients where we lived. Home was private.

"Well," I said, setting my backpack on the ground as I sank into my client chair. "How can I help you?"

"Why did my sister come to you?"

I reached sideways into my backpack to make sure the grip end of my blackjack was at the ready. Then I dug around for an old napkin, pulled one out, and took my time wiping off the bottom of my cup.

Oliver drummed his fingers on the arm of my chair. He was not a patient boy.

"I don't work for you," I said after a good, long while. "I can't tell you that."

His lips pinched tight.

"I'd advise you to reconsider," he said. "You don't know what you're dealing with, and I'd hate for you to get hurt."

"I almost never know what I'm dealing with. Keeps me sharp," I said. "Why do *you* think she hired me?"

His right eyelid twitched. "I couldn't say."

"Well, then I guess we don't have a lot to talk about." I took a sip of cocoa. A vein on his neck pulsed. I took another sip. The vein pulsed faster.

"Was there anything else, Oliver?"

He scowled. Jerked his legs off my desk and sat up straight. As he did, I saw that the cuffs of his shirt were buttoned around his wrists, tight as a fat man's belt.

"I want you to tell me why my sister is staying with my aunt. I'm her brother. I have a right to know!"

I smiled, sweet as could be. "Look at you, all worried about Gemma. Tell me, is that *her* name carved into your wrist? I mean, tattoos are dandy, but nothing says 'I love you' like a good scar."

He stood up so fast the chair skidded into the wall behind it. "You'll regret this," he growled.

"Seriously?" I said. "That's the line you're going with? 'You'll regret this'?"

He gave me a look meant to freeze my heart. "You won't be so smug for long," he spat. "Consider yourself warned."

"Consider it considered."

He stomped across the room, shot me one last withering look, and slammed the door so hard I thought the glass would shatter.

It held.

I drank some more cocoa. Got up. And went around to my own chair, where I belonged.

10

An hour later I was still at my desk, watching the morning unfold down on Carroll Street. Families dressed in their Sunday best strolled home from church. Sleepy-eyed heathens straggled out of the bodega across the street with newspapers and coffee. On the computer behind me, the Library of Alexandria's website was open to a picture of *Abbi*'s bottle.

Only it wasn't actually one of his; it was an exact replica owned by the Egyptian government.

BOTTLE, CIRCA 950 BC, the caption read. HELD IN STORAGE. Below that were links to three academic papers. The first argued that the bottle was nothing more than a souvenir made for early spice traders to take home to their wives.

Not so interesting.

The second was better.

Its authors had used carbon dating and some kind of metallurgical analysis to figure out that the bottle was made in Jerusalem during the reign of King Suleyman, a.k.a. Solomon, a.k.a. the guy with the knot. They'd tried to open it, since every archaeologist and engineer who'd seen the thing swore its lid was designed to come off. But that hadn't worked out so well, and in the end, all they could say was that the bottle was old.

And the third paper? Well, that's where things got interesting. According to Ebe Sawalha, PhD, the bottle on display in Egypt hadn't just been cast during Solomon's reign; it was made *for* the guy. She said the design on the lid was an impression made by Solomon's own ring, which, according to some legends, was what gave him the power to control humans and jinn, animals and weather. Devout Muslims believed Solomon's power came from Allah, but Dr. Sawalha's research had turned up ancient texts describing a magical ring that, when used in conjunction with a bottle called the *Shubaak*, allowed Solomon to imprison rebellious jinn.

According to those same texts, the *Shubaak*'s lid could only be removed by someone who both possessed the ring and knew the proper incantation to say over it. The ring, Dr. Sawalha wrote, had disappeared after Solomon's death. And the incantation had been lost to time.

I rotated the Alexandria bottle's picture through its 360-degree view and saw that the bottom was smooth. If *Abbi* had been right about only the hash marked bottle being the real deal, then the museum copy was a fake. Which meant my dad's family of quiet, bookish Egyptians had somehow ended up with an antiquity so precious that a *copy* of it was on display in a museum. Which meant that some ancient king's super-special-magic-and-unicorns *Shubaak* was, at that very moment, sitting in a steel box on Fourth Street at the central branch of the Las Almas Teachers Credit Union.

How the hell had that happened?

While my brain tangled with this brand-new mystery, my eyes watched the conspicuously inconspicuous woman down on Carroll Street. She'd been there since Oliver left, leaning against the bricks of a doorway four buildings over, using a newspaper to hide her face. As I watched, the paper dropped low enough for me to see her.

Blondie.

My tail from yesterday.

A few seconds later, I spotted her dark-haired buddy huddling under a ratty coat, holding out a hand to collect change from passersby. The General hadn't put in an appearance yet that morning, but any panhandler worth her salt would know better than to set up shop on his turf. That, along with the fact that she kept looking up at my window every few minutes, gave Shorty away.

The day before, my shadows hadn't made a secret of their tail job. They'd wanted me to see them, wanted me scared. Staying hidden meant the game had changed. I wasn't just a nuisance anymore. I was a threat.

I took out my phone and hit Gemma's number. I hadn't heard from her in a while, and with Oliver out making unwanted social calls, and me pissing him off even more than he'd been before, I wanted to know she was safe. More importantly, I wanted to make sure she stayed that way. The kid was turning me soft.

One ring did the trick.

"Hi, Scarlett."

"Hey," I said. "Everything good with you?"

"Good enough. Did you figure out what's going on?"

I kept my eye on Blondie. "Sort of, but I've got a long way to go."

"That's okay," she said. "Aunt Lucy likes it when I help out with my cousin, Knox. He can't talk yet. He's fun."

I smiled in spite of myself. I'd only known Gemma for a day, but she was smart enough to know what was what.

"I'm glad, kid," I said. "Listen, you sit tight, be careful, and shoot me a text every once in a while to let me know you're hanging in there. And don't leave your aunt's place except for school. Honestly, I wish you didn't have to go out at all, but if you start skipping or faking sick, your parents might figure out there's something going on."

"Sure," she said. "And, Scarlett?"

"Yeah?"

"You be careful, too."

I closed my computer. "Don't worry about me, kid. I'll be fine."

She said good-bye. I did the same and called Emmet Morales.

He took three rings.

"Scarlett?"

"Morning, Emmet. How's my favorite cop?"

"You know me—I'm always good. Haven't heard from you in a while, though. Keeping your nose clean?"

"Clean*ish*."

Trouble wasn't a topic to joke about with Emmet. I did it anyway.

"What's up?" he said.

"I was hoping we could meet sometime today."

"New client?"

"Nah. I just miss your pretty face."

"Yeah. Right. Tell me about the case."

I laughed. Tried to sound casual.

"It's nothing special. Just a little girl with a brother who's been acting weird lately. Staying out too much, getting into fights, that kind of thing. Oh, and one of his friends took a little tumble Friday."

"Keep going," Emmet said

"The friend was Quinlan Johnson."

I could picture him in the silence that followed, folding his lower lip in with his index finger and thumb, thinking.

"A lot of bad stuff goes down on the streets," he said after a while. "Sounds like this kid needs a shrink more than a detective. I know some good ones. How about I give you a name?"

He sounded guarded. Careful.

"You know," I said, "I might just take you up on that once I sort out some other stuff. Like why my client's brother broke into my office this morning and tried to scare me off the case."

"Tried to scare you how?"

"Tough talk. Nothing big."

"Families get messed up, Scarlett. You don't know what this kid might have tangled with or what's going on in his sister's head. Maybe she's just trying to get him in trouble. Did you talk to the parents?"

"She says they're out to lunch, and so far everything else she's told me has checked out."

"Maybe she's just looking for attention. How'd she get your name?"

"Business card in the school bathroom."

He laughed. "Quite the entrepreneur, aren't you?"

"Don't change the subject. Can we meet or not?"

"Being police is a real job, you know. I don't have time to play sidekick to some ghetto Nancy Drew."

His words sounded cruel, but I knew better.

"I'll remember that the next time you need my help tracking down a serial killer, *Detective* Morales."

"I suppose you do come in handy once in a while," he said, laughing again.

"So how about Rita Mae's?" I asked. "Say, in an hour?"

"Sure. Rita Mae's."

"Great. Oh, and Emmet, what can you tell me about Quinlan Johnson?"

The line went quiet.

"Emmet?"

"It's not my case," he said.

"That's not what I asked."

"I know."

"So you'll tell me what you can?"

"Rita Mae's," Emmet said. He wasn't laughing anymore. "See you there."

✖

Blondie and Shorty hadn't budged, and since I wasn't in the mood for company, there was no choice but to ditch them the hard way. I tucked my blackjack under my jacket sleeve, strapped my bag across my chest, and hit the street.

Blondie stayed behind her paper as I passed by. I didn't look up, didn't let on that I knew she was there. I stopped at the curb, snuck a peek at Shorty, and crossed to the newsstand on the other side of the street.

A curved security mirror was mounted up high on the stand's wall. I grabbed a magazine, snuck a peek at the mirror, caught Blondie pretending to read a flyer on a lamppost. Farther back, Shorty was still holding out her cup to passersby. I put down the magazine, bought a pack of gum, and strolled two blocks east to Zelinski's Bagel Shop. Sundays were always busy there, and since my tails were doing their best to stay invisible, with any luck they wouldn't follow me in.

It worked. Inside the shop, counter workers jitter-bugged back and forth along a row of overflowing metal baskets, tossing bagels and bialys into paper bags, slapping spackling knives full of cream cheese into tubs. Cashiers shouted orders and rang up sales so fast the registers smoked. Any other morning, I would have taken time to be impressed.

I made my way to the front of the line, using a tall man in a Windbreaker for cover. After a few minutes, I turned and pretended to look at the clock over the door. Blondie was peering in the window. She seemed anxious, like her puppy had wandered too far away in the park. I pulled a handful of pennies out of my pocket, let them fall to the floor in a patter of *clink*s. Then I crouched low, crawling through the crowd as I pretended to gather them, muttering "excuse me" and working my way toward the narrow passage that staff used to get behind the counter. No one noticed when I crawled under and snuck back to the kitchen. And even if the counter workers had, they'd have been too busy to care.

In the hot, calm back room, a mountain of a man dumping salt bagels off a peel saw me making tracks along the wall.

"Morning, Scarlett. Who'd you piss off today?"

"Nobody good, Edgar."

I kept moving.

"One of these days somebody's gonna wise up to your little escape route. Till then I might have to start charging a toll each time you cut through here."

"Yeah, well, if I make it to next time, you can name your price," I said.

Edgar laughed.

"Heads up!" He chucked a hot bagel toward my noggin. I caught it on the fly and told him I owed him one.

"One?" he called after me.

"Maybe two," I hollered back, and started down the basement stairs.

At the bottom, I cut right and ran to the heavy double doors that led up to the street. I lifted the right-hand side, scanned the alley, saw it was empty except for a crook-tailed cat licking his paw on a Dumpster. I climbed out, closed the door behind me, and hightailed it to the nearest metro station, stopping at the turnstiles to make sure my tails hadn't caught on to my trick. I checked again at the top of the platform stairs and once more from behind a stained tile column near the tracks. The coast stayed clear, but after what had happened the day before, I knew better than to be smug or lazy. In my business, smug and lazy got you in trouble.

And sometimes they even got you dead.

11

Emmet wasn't at the restaurant when I arrived, so I got a table and took out *Abbi*'s copy of *One Thousand and One Nights*. It smelled of leather and dust and things I couldn't have, and made me miss my parents so bad it hurt.

I opened it to the first page. Traced the outline of a water stain. Ran my finger over an indigo inscription I hadn't remembered was there: *Abd al-Malik.*

Servant of the King.

"You ready to order yet?"

My waitress stood a few feet away, and judging by the look on her face, she wasn't any too pleased about it. She was only a year or two older than me, but her kitchen-sink bleach job, pockmarked skin, and blood-shot eyes all told me life had dealt her a rough hand.

"My friend will be here soon," I said. "Can I get a soda while I wait?"

She sniffed and meandered away. I doubted I'd see her anytime soon.

Then Emmet walked in.

Emmet was tall and broad shouldered, with blue-black skin, black-brown eyes, and neat little dreads all over his head. His ironed white shirt looked crisp under a camel-hair jacket, and other than the barely legal spring-assisted knife he carried in a strap around his right calf, his jeans weren't keeping any secrets.

"You're early," he said.

"You're not."

I smiled. Seeing Emmet always reminded me that I wished I could see him more.

He hung his jacket on the hook at the end of the booth and sat down.

"Been waiting long?"

"Long enough to cheese off Miss Sunshine over there."

"That sweet thing?" Emmet grinned at the hard-faced girl as she hustled toward us.

"Afternoon, Detective. What can I get for you?" She was suddenly all smiles.

"Apart from your lovely self?" he said. "How about a cup of coffee?" The waitress giggled, then hustled off to get the coffee.

Emmet had first introduced Reem and me to Rita Mae's two years earlier. That had been a good meal. A great meal, really, since he'd just managed to convince an old bulldog of a judge not to send me to Hammett House. "The food here tastes like my granny cooked it," he'd said. To me, a fourteen-year-old kid who'd just dodged a stretch in the worst juvy lockup in the state, Rita Mae's food tasted like freedom.

But our friendship with Emmet hadn't started off so happy. He'd still been a beat cop the day he and a washed-out homicide detective showed up on our doorstep to tell us *Abbi* was dead. And he'd made a lousy show of looking tough, sitting stiff as starch on our couch while the detective droned on and on and on. After that, he'd driven *Ummi* and Reem and me to the morgue in his squad car. He went into the observation room with *Ummi*, too, and all but carried her out when she was done.

From then on, Emmet kept in touch with a call here, a ring on the doorbell there. He cared, so we cared back. *Ummi* cooked for him and fussed over his weight and loved him like a son. When she died, he'd helped carry her shrouded body to its grave. He hadn't looked tough then, either. He hadn't even bothered trying.

So when I got busted hot-wiring a Lexus in ninth grade, Reem had called him straightaway. He stayed with me through booking, called in favors to get my paperwork moving, and promised the judge he'd keep me on the straight and narrow.

And he had, mainly by putting me to work. At first I only helped with little things: seeing if liquor stores would sell to me with a fake ID, digging up records at City Hall, scouting for pickpockets in tourist areas. Turned out I had a knack for talking to people and the natural stubbornness it took to be a gumshoe. So Emmet taught me how to tail suspects, run surveillance, and work a case. He even got the owner of his muay Thai gym to train me for free, and pretended not to know I'd forged Reem's signature on the gym's release forms. "I can't send you out there like a lamb to the slaughter," he'd muttered under his breath. "It wouldn't be right."

From then on, he'd brought me in on juvy cases where an inside angle might help move things along. I was young. I wasn't a cop. That meant I could go places cops couldn't and get teenagers to talk to me. The arrangement wasn't official. Hell, it wasn't even kosher. But Emmet had a soft spot for kids, and I had a soft spot for Emmet. We made it work.

While Emmet sipped his coffee, I filled him in as best I could on my life. Yes, I was still working cases. No, I wasn't doing anything too dangerous. No, I hadn't gotten any taller.

He listened close, asking questions when it suited him.

"How's Reem?" he said, nodding a thank-you to the waitress for refilling his cup. I'd given up on my soda.

"Busy."

"She taking care of herself?"

"Not really."

Emmet took the wrapper off a straw and rolled it into a ball.

"You helping out?"

"As much as I can. I keep the apartment clean and make sure she eats."

He poured a plastic container of cream into his coffee and stirred.

"Tell her I said hello. And if she ever has a night off…"

He let the words hover.

"You know Muslim women can't date, Emmet," I said. "And Reem's hard-core. Unless that changes, it just won't work."

He smiled and shrugged like he didn't care. Only I knew he did.

"How about some pie, handsome?" The waitress was back, and she wasn't talking to me.

"What kind you got?" He draped his arm over the back of the seat. Emmet was not unaware of his charms.

"The usuals, plus boysenberry and mango."

"I think I'll take chocolate cream with a slice of peach on the side. If I've got room after that, I'll try the mango."

"Anything else?" Her lashes looked ready to flutter off her face.

Emmet looked to me. The waitress did not.

"I'd like a slice of sweet potato," I said. "And my soda, if you don't mind." Her pen moved across the pad in her hand, but her eyes stayed on Emmet. She batted her lashes one last time and walked away, rear end swinging.

I pretended to throw up in my mouth. Emmet grinned.

"I can't help it, Scarlett."

"Yes. You can."

He laughed, eyeing the waitress like a well-fed wolf. "Maybe a little. But there's no point behaving till I've got someone worth doing it for."

I rolled my eyes. Asked him if we could talk about something more important.

"Nothing's more important than you and your sister."

I rolled them some more.

"Tell me about Quinlan Johnson."

His smile disappeared like a raindrop in the ocean. "Like I said on the phone, it sounds like your client's brother needs counseling, not a detective."

"Maybe," I said. "But my *client* needs me."

We watched the waitress set three fat wedges of pie in front of Emmet and slap my soda down. "The mango's on the house," she said, giving Emmet a wink. "I made it myself. Tell me if I put in enough sugar."

"Darlin', if it's half as sweet as you, it's twice as sweet as I can handle."

She let out a quackish giggle and waggled back to her station like a duck in heat. I didn't bother wondering if my pie would ever show.

"Emmet," I asked quietly. "Were there any marks on Quinlan Johnson's body?"

His fork froze halfway to his mouth.

"Yes."

"Well?"

"What kind of marks do you mean?"

"Tattoos. Scars. Stuff like that."

He put the forkful of chocolate in his mouth and chewed a long time before he swallowed.

"Maybe."

"Was there a kind of design, like interlocking rings?"

"Maybe."

"I'll take that as a yes."

Emmet put down his fork. "What makes you ask?"

"Well, I'm pretty sure my client's brother has the same thing carved into his wrist. It's red and infected and ugly, and he's not doing anything to keep it clean. Like he wants it to scar."

Emmet pushed the chocolate pie away.

"There *was* a mark on the Johnson boy's body, exactly like the one you're describing. The medical examiner said it was at least three weeks old."

"On his wrist?"

"Chest. We think it's a ritual mark from some kind of gang or cult that hasn't crossed our radar until now."

"A rich white boy gang?"

"Or cult," Emmet repeated. "That's what I'm thinking. The department psychologist, too."

"Why?"

Emmet mulled over his response. He wasn't going to spill everything, but he wasn't going to leave me hanging.

"From what the boy's parents told us, he'd been very involved with a new group of friends in the past few months. Apparently they were playing some kind of elaborate, real-life fantasy game together."

"Had the parents been worried?"

"They said yes, but I'm not so sure. You know how it goes." He pressed his lips together and pulled the slice of mango closer.

"Emmet?"

"Mmmm?"

"Quinn Johnson's father is second-in-command at Archer Construction. My client's name is Archer. Gemma Archer."

His eyes narrowed.

"You know anything about all the problems with The Parker?" I asked.

He took a mouthful of mango and grimaced. "Too much sugar."

"Let's stick to The Parker," I said. "The *Globe* mentioned four break-ins at Archer Construction's on-site trailer."

Emmet sighed. "Five. The last was an inside job. Whoever did it had a key, but they weren't authorized to go in after hours. The company wanted that one kept quiet."

"Did the thieves take anything?"

"The first four times? No. They just tore the place up. Spray-painted walls and such."

"With interlocking rings?"

Emmet nodded and scowled at his pie like it was trying to get away.

"What about the fifth?"

He took another bite and grimaced again. "Still too sweet."

"Emmet?"

"Robbery's not my department, Scarlett. I'm in homicide, remember?"

"Look," I said. "I think there's more to Quinn Johnson's death than suicide, and I need your help proving it."

He folded in his lower lip.

"You're stalling," I said.

"You're right." He dropped his hand and nodded, more for himself than me. "The thieves took a stack of papers from the secretary's out-box."

105

"Any idea why?"

Emmet's lips curled into a lopsided smile. "You're the detective. You tell me."

"Funny."

"It kind of was," he said. "But the truth is, we're not sure why. All they got was opened mail that the secretary hadn't had a chance to sort. Invoices. Receipts. Stuff like that. The only thing she hadn't laid eyeballs on directly was an unopened envelope that needed forwarding to The Parker's architect in Chicago."

I pushed my glass around, spreading the little puddle of condensation underneath it.

"She didn't have any idea what was in it?" I asked.

"Nope."

"Are you telling me everything?"

Emmet sat back and crossed his arms over his chest. "In case you haven't noticed, Scarlett, I don't like it when kids get lost in the system. I'm trying to help you here."

I gave him a smile for that. A real one.

"I know. You're a good guy, Emmet."

"Don't believe it for a minute." He noticed the empty space in front of me and started to wave the waitress over. "You didn't get your pie."

106

"Stop," I said. Emmet took one look at my face and waved her off. She wilted like week-old flowers.

"I don't want pie," I said. "I want to figure out what happened to Quinn Johnson. The *Globe* said he threw something that looked like paper into the water before he jumped. Do you know what it was?"

"Here." Emmet pushed the wedge of peach toward me. "I can't eat three."

"Emmet?" I shoved the plate back.

He took in a long breath and let it out through pursed lips.

"No. We don't know what it was."

"Then what did he say to the woman on the bridge before he jumped?"

Emmet's body coiled up tight as an overwound music box.

"Emmet?"

He jiggled his coffee cup back and forth by the handle.

"You're not as tough as you think, Scarlett," he said.

"Probably not."

"And you've got a lot to learn."

"I know."

"No. You don't." He shook his head slowly back and forth. "You really don't."

I took a bite of pie to try to flush the taste of condescension out of my mouth. It didn't work.

"Emmet, what did Quinn say before he jumped?"

His brown eyes filled with pain, like they had after *Abbi* died.

"Promise you'll come to me for help if you get in over your head with this one?" he said.

"I promise."

His voice went rough.

"Quinn said, 'Sam's safe now.' And then he jumped."

"That's all?"

The pain in Emmet's eyes darkened down to something more like anger. "That's all. But you know, Scarlett, I think something—someone—*made* that boy kill himself. The coroner ruled it a suicide, though, so I can't do a damned thing about it. At least not officially."

I reached for his hand, wondering what the hell was up with me and all the hand-holding lately.

It was more than our waitress could stand. She sashayed over to ask if we wanted anything else. Emmet ignored her and looked up at the ceiling. I told her we were set. She tossed the bill on the table and left in a huff.

"Don't worry, Emmet," I said, giving his hand a squeeze before I picked up the check. "This one's on me."

12

The address Emmet gave me for Quinn Johnson's family put them in a part of town where the right bank account bought you a prime view of Christie Park. A doorman sat just inside the lobby of their building, watching his phone with one eye and the street with the other. Doormen could be a brick wall or your best friend depending on how you played them. I turned around, hoofed it six blocks north to a flower shop, and came back.

From the way he studied me before he even looked at the bouquet of purple dahlias in my hand, I could tell the guy knew his stuff. Good doormen, the ones worth their holiday tips, always checked faces first.

"These are for the Johnsons," I said, keeping my eyes wide and innocent. "I'm Scarlett. I was a friend of Quinlan's at Chandler Academy."

He gave a sad nod.

"Awful thing," he said. "Just awful. Hold on a sec."

He picked up an old-fashioned intercom receiver and punched in an apartment number.

"There's a young lady down here with flowers," he said. "Says she knew Quinn. Shall I send her up?"

He looked me over some more while the person on the other end talked.

"Sure thing." He put the receiver back on its hook. "They aren't taking visitors right now, sweetheart, but you can leave your posies with me, and I'll make sure they get where they're supposed to."

I blinked a few times and made my smile extra innocent.

"Actually," I said, "I'm kind of relieved. I was nervous about seeing them. Didn't want to say the wrong thing, you know? Paying my respects just seemed like the right thing to do."

I started to hand him the flowers. Stopped midreach.

"Say," I said, as if the thought had just hit me. "Sam isn't home, is he? I should check on him, see how he's doing."

The doorman got a soft look on his face and nodded. "Lemme check."

He picked up the receiver to try again, gave me a smile and a wink as he talked.

Pay dirt.

"Housekeeper says Sam's coming down," the doorman said when he was through. "She thinks it'd do him good to see a friend."

"Oh." I shifted my smile from wistful to relieved. "That's great!" I gave the door a drawn-out glance. "You know, it's such a beautiful day, I think I'll wait for him outside."

"Good idea." Half the doorman's attention had already drifted back to his phone. "I'll send him your way."

"Thanks," I said.

He tipped his hat. I gave him one last dazzling smile.

Playing it nice had been the right call after all.

Sam Johnson was short, round, and topped off with a shock of indignant red hair. He walked fast, like he'd made up his mind about something and wanted the world to know it.

"Did they send you?" He was all fury, and dangerous as a bad case of hiccups.

"My name's Scarlett," I said. "I'm so sorry about your brother."

He planted his fists on his hips. "They *did*, didn't they? Well, you tell them they can all just go to hell!" The freckles across his cheeks merged into angry red blotches.

"Wait a minute," I said. "I'm not sure who you think I am, but how about we start over?"

He glared at me like an angry garden gnome.

"I'm Scarlett," I said, handing him one of my cards. "I'm a private detective, and I work for Gemma Archer. You know her, right?"

He looked at the card.

"This is from the crapper at school!"

I smiled, bright and encouraging. "That's right. I put some in the restrooms there to drum up business."

"You're not from the Ch—I mean, you're really not one of them?"

"I don't know who 'them' is, Sam. Like I told you, Gemma hired me to help her. Maybe I can help you, too."

He eyed me warily. "Did you put the cards in the boys' bathroom yourself?"

"I did."

"You'd have been toast if Stokes caught you."

"Is he the security guard at Chandler?"

"Uh-huh." Sam sounded wary now, but his fury was fading. Defying Stokes had earned me some cred.

"I had lots of practice dodging guys like him when I was in school," I said. "It was good training for what I do now."

"Where'd you go?"

"Mosley."

"They've got a good basketball team."

"Yeah. The best."

He frowned and shook his head like he was reminding himself not to trust me. "How do I know you're not one of them?"

"Honestly, Sam, I can't answer that until you tell me who 'them' is."

He looked up and down the street and back again.

"You really don't know?"

"I really don't. Gemma came to me because her brother..."

"Oliver." Sam spat the name out like sour milk.

"Right. Gemma came to me because Oliver's been acting funny lately. She said he had a fight with Quinn at school. That's why I wanted to talk to you. I thought you might know what was going on between the two of them."

"Everyone thinks Quinn killed himself. Even my mom and dad." Sam looked down at his feet and scuffed at the concrete.

"What do *you* think, Sam?"

His eyes lifted, full of raw hurt.

"My brother wouldn't ever do that. Not unless someone made him."

"I think you're right," I said.

His forehead smoothed out. His fists unclenched.

"You do?"

"Uh-huh."

"And the Children of Iblis didn't send you?"

I thought back to Emmet's cult theory. In Islam, Iblis was an evil jinn who defied Allah. He was *Shaytan*. The devil. Maybe a group of nut balls out there had latched on and started worshipping him or some such.

"They didn't send me," I said. "I've never even heard of them. Is that who Quinn had been hanging around with lately? The Children of Iblis?"

Sam ran the toe of his sneaker along a crack in the sidewalk and nodded.

"You know," I said, "it would really help me if I knew more about them."

"Help you how?"

"I want to figure out what made Quinn do what he did, and I want to keep Gemma safe. A lot of weird stuff has been happening in this town. It needs to stop."

"What kind of weird stuff?" Sam asked.

"Well, for one thing, two women have been following me ever since I met Oliver."

"Do they have gold rings in their eyes?"

My pulse started jumping rope.

"Yes. Have you seen them before?"

"No, but..."

His voice faded to nothing.

"Are they part of the Children of Iblis, Sam?"

He nodded. "I think so."

"Can you tell me how Quinn got involved with them?"

Sam hesitated, but not for long.

"It started at Xeno's Paradise. That's an arcade with real old games like *Pac-Man* and *Galaga* and stuff. Quinn liked hanging out there. You know it?"

I said I didn't.

He scrunched up his lips. "Anyway, one day he came home all excited about how this really hot girl with gold rings in her eyes had come over to watch him play *Street Fighter* and stuck around afterward to talk. She let him take her out for pizza. That's when she told him about the Children of Iblis. She said their games were way better than the ones at Xeno's."

He paused, nervous.

"Did she say why?" I asked

"Uh-huh. They do real-life role-playing games."

"Like *Dungeons and Dragons*?"

"No. That's pretend. The Children of Iblis go on quests for real things in the real world."

"Like what, Sam?"

"Like this old ring that supposedly belonged to a king from the Bible. And some bottle Quinn called a *shooba*."

My pulse switched to double Dutch. "Was it maybe a *Shubaak*?"

He shrugged. "Maybe. Anyway, Quinn said he

wanted to join, so the girl started texting him little missions. Fun stuff, like scavenger hunts to antique shops. He took me along sometimes."

"What was her name, Sam?"

"Quinn wouldn't tell me. Members' names are supposed to be secret. I knew about Oliver, though."

"What did you know about him?"

"I heard Quinn on the phone one night telling Oliver how awesome the Children of Iblis were. He said they'd asked if he and Oliver were friends, and did he think Oliver would join them. I could tell Oliver didn't want to at first. He's kind of a dick."

"I'm with you on that one, kid," I said.

The sheepish look on his face melted into a short, sweet smile that lasted only until he spoke.

"So Quinn talked Oliver into joining, but after a few weeks he told me he wished he hadn't. He said that with Oliver there, it was like they forgot all about him."

"The Children of Iblis forgot all about Quinn?"

"Yeah." Sam's mouth scrunched up again. "After that he stopped talking to me about them and started going out all the time. He was acting really strange. Scared, even."

"Your dad works for Archer Construction, right?" I said.

"Yeah."

"Does he keep a lot of work stuff at home?"

"Some, I guess." He did the scrunchy lip thing again. It was a cute tic. He probably hated it.

"Can you tell me anything more?" I asked.

His shoulders slumped. "You mind if we sit down?"

I steered us over to a nearby bench. As we sat, the slump spread to the rest of his body.

"You okay, Sam?"

He nodded. Looked at the ground. "Yeah."

I scooted closer and bumped him with my elbow. His eyes lifted. Searched mine. Found whatever it was he'd needed to keep going.

"So one day Dad came home really upset because someone had broken into his office at The Parker site."

"Did he say if they took anything?"

Sam shrank into himself and dropped his voice so low I could barely hear him.

"No."

He was holding something back.

"Sam?"

He looked so scared I wanted to hug him and make it go away.

"I'm going to help you, kid."

He sniffled.

"Quinn did it."

"Did what?"

Sam swiped at his face with his sleeve and mumbled something I couldn't make out.

"What?"

"Quinn broke into the trailer, okay? He's the one who did it!" Sam shouted. Waves of pain and anger rolled off his rigid body like heat from a furnace.

Emmet had said it was an inside job—that whoever broke in had used a key but wasn't authorized to be there after hours. I moved away from Sam on the bench. Gave him space. Time. And slowly, slowly, he came back to me.

"Sorry," he croaked.

"Don't be," I said. "You've got every right to be mad."

"I do?" He was exhausted.

"Hell yes. If my sister got sucked in by these Children of Iblis people, I'd be more than mad. I'd want to destroy them."

He sat up taller.

"You would?"

"I would."

He watched a pigeon peck at a stray candy wrapper. I waited.

It paid off.

"I saw something in Quinn's room," he said. "A note. From the guy who's building The Parker."

I thought back to the *Globe* articles I'd dug up, found the guy's name filed away in my brain under "Stuff I Shouldn't Forget."

"George Fagin?" I asked.

"Uh-huh."

"What did it say?" I didn't speak gently, didn't baby him. We were allies, Sam and I.

"Not much. It was a thank-you note to an architect for blueprints he'd done."

"What were the blueprints for?"

"A new wing for some old building. That's all the note said."

"Do you remember the architect's name?"

"Nope." He shook his head.

"Was there a return address?"

"Uh-uh. I didn't see the envelope, and the note wasn't typed or anything. It was really short. Fagin wrote it himself."

"Where's the letter now, Sam?"

He got quiet again, but he didn't shut down.

"I think Quinn took it with him to the bridge."

I gave the moment time to breathe and braced for the hardest question of all.

"Why did Quinn go to the bridge, Sam?"

His voice broke as he spoke, but Sam did not.

"He went because of me."

"How do you know that?"

Sam shuddered. "The day it happened, I heard a text alert go off in Quinn's room. He was in Dad's office with the door shut and couldn't hear. I snuck in and read it."

"What did the text say, Sam?"

A sob shook his body. I put my arm around him and shot a dirty look at the woman staring at us from the sidewalk.

"If I give you Quinn's phone," Sam said, his words coming out in hitched little bursts, "you'll get them, right? You'll get the Children of Iblis and prove my brother didn't want to kill himself?"

I hugged him tighter.

"Yeah, Sam. I'll get them," I promised. "I'll get them."

13

I liked the library near our apartment, liked hanging out with schoolkids and homeless people and moms with toddlers, all of us breathing in the smell of old varnish and ideas. I liked the librarians who were happy to help you. I even liked the ones who weren't. It was the kind of place where you could lose yourself, which was why I went there after my visit with Sam.

The best spot in the whole joint was a dusty room on the top floor filled with rows and rows of flat, wide drawers. Each held a map, along with the promise of someplace better. Melvin, the room's librarian, nodded at me when I walked in. I gave him a wave and went straight to my favorite drawer.

Inside it, the world on paper was as beautiful as ever. I ran the tip of my finger from Las Almas all the way across the Atlantic, south through Africa and the Indian Ocean, to Bali. Bali was where I went when things got too crazy. I closed my eyes, pictured blue water, white sand, the feel of sun on my skin. It was always quiet in Bali. And with any luck, if what *Ummi* and *Abbi* had taught me about *Qadar* was true, maybe I was destined to end up there someday.

The funny thing was, I'd always been a skeptic when it came to *Qadar*. I didn't like the idea that everything was already set, that no matter what choices I made, my path through life had been mapped out a long time ago. But ever since Gemma had shown up at my door, fate had yanked the steering wheel from my hands and hit the gas pedal hard. This case wasn't just about some rich kid getting messed up by a cult. It was about old devils and new ones. It was about my faith. My family. About me.

Melvin sneezed loud enough to cut my trip short. I opened my eyes, caught him watching me. He went back to his book. I said good-bye to Bali, sat down in front of the room's only computer, took out Quinn

Johnson's phone, and pulled up the last text he'd ever received.

Sam will pay. And we will find Fagin.

That was the message from Oliver that Sam had intercepted, the one that scared him bad enough to make him hide his brother's phone to show his parents. Only Quinn had left before they got home. Left for good.

Every other text on the phone had been deleted, except for the one Quinn had sent to Oliver half an hour earlier.

It won't do you any good to go after Sam.

I won't help you open the portal.

You can't have the letter. You can't have me.

I plugged Oliver's number into my own address book so I'd know it if he called. Checked Quinn's email folder. Cursed when it came up empty. Melvin gave me the evil eye.

"Sorry," I said, even though I wasn't. Quinn had scrubbed his phone clean. No mail, no other texts. But thanks to Sam, I knew the Children of Iblis were after Solomon's ring, *Abbi*'s *Shubaak*, and a rich guy named George Fagin.

It was a start.

I switched to the computer and ran a search.

124

Thousands of hits came back for the name George Fagin, but the more I went through them, the more I knew there was a whole lot of nothing there. *Reclusive. Elusive. Mysterious.* Those words showed up a lot. *Billionaire*, too. George Fagin didn't give interviews and wouldn't communicate directly with the press. Hell, he'd never even been *seen*. From what I could tell, the guy was a pro at three things: making money, giving it away, and keeping the whole wide world from finding out a damned thing about him.

No matter how many newspaper articles and bits of gossip column trash I read, each hit seemed to say less than the one before it. My eyes got so bleary I could barely see. *One more*, I thought, clicking on a link that read REWARD FOR FAGIN.

The page loaded.

A long whistle slipped through my teeth before I could stop it. Melvin looked ready to pass a kitten. "*Shh!*" he hissed.

Black words stood out against the screen's bloodred background.

FIND GEORGE FAGIN
MILLION DOLLAR REWARD

Underneath that was a thick-lined image of Solomon's knot, and, at the bottom of the page, in smaller letters:

The Children of Iblis

"Melvin," I said, "if I were a millionaire, would you run away to Bali with me?"

Melvin put his book down and gave me his scariest librarian glare.

I told him I'd thought that was what he'd say.

He scowled. I got up.

"It's your call, Mel, but you'll be sorry when all you have to remember me by is a postcard."

He scowled some more.

I smiled, blew him a kiss, and walked out, thinking what a good thing we had, Melvin and me. It was simple. Straightforward. Easy. And nothing—nothing at all— like the complicated world outside the library doors.

Out on the street, the wind had picked up, and Decker was on my mind. I hadn't called or texted since the night before, because I wanted him keeping track of me like I wanted a fresh paper cut. But it had been a hard day, and I needed him, needed to *feel* his voice, not just hear it. To breathe in the soap and spice smells of him. For that, a phone call wouldn't do.

I hoofed a circle two blocks wide around the Laundromat in case my tails were still there and headed north to the Rubicon. Deck usually worked the dinner shift on Sundays. With any luck, things would be busy enough for me to slip into the kitchen unnoticed. Just thinking about being next to him in the warm, tight space was enough to nudge me into a jog.

But when I got there and saw the General sitting in a room full of empty tables, I knew straight off that luck wasn't doing me any favors that night. The General looked up from his meal, the one Delilah fed him every Sunday for free, and gave me a cheery wave through the window.

"Hey, General," I said, pushing open the door. "What's cooking?"

He never had a chance to answer. Delilah barreled out of the kitchen like a one-woman stampede.

"Scarlett!" She pulled me into a hug so tight I couldn't talk. "You're here!"

I saw our reflection in the front window, Delilah,

short and sturdy, me all arms and legs. I looked surprised as hell.

"Play along," she whispered in my ear. "Manny will explain everything tomorrow."

Right after that, Reem came through the kitchen door, looking more relaxed than I'd seen her in a long time.

Delilah squeezed me even tighter. "The less Reem knows, the safer she'll be."

"I thought you were working tonight," I said, flashing Reem a happy-to-see-you smile as Delilah finally let go.

My sister rolled her eyes. "I told you last week they changed my schedule, Lettie. For a detective, you've sure got a lousy memory."

"Right," I said, glancing back at the kitchen. Delilah noticed.

"Decker went home, hon," she said. "Things were too quiet to make him stay."

I was trapped, and I'd done it to myself.

"But I'm so glad you're here," Delilah went on. "Because I owe the two of you an apology."

My lips clamped down just in time to keep me from smarting off, asking if the weather service had just issued a frost warning in hell.

"Like I was telling Reem," Delilah said, "I've been in an awful state since my ex showed up again. Deck's father, I mean."

I started to point out that Deck's father was dead, but Delilah cut me off.

"I know," she said. "I've always let folks assume he died. But that was just my way of not having to think about him. See, he's the sort that won't leave ancient history alone, and I try to keep him away from Decker as much as I can. From the both of you, too. He was a friend of your folks once upon a time, but he's got no business bothering either one of you now."

Reem was watching Delilah with the intensely sympathetic look I imagined she got when she listened to her patients. It was no wonder they all loved her.

"Not that he's a bad man, of course," Delilah said. "Though I suppose he can come across that way. Truth is, Asim's one of the good guys. He's just a little hard to take."

Asim.

The name spun through my head like a blown-out tire. Asim was Delilah's ex. Delilah's ex was Decker's father. Decker's father had broken into our apartment the night before and stolen *Abbi*'s bottle replica, which was somehow tied up with King Solomon and his missing ring and George Fagin and Quinn Johnson's death. What the hell was going on?

Delilah shot me a look meant to keep me quiet. I was too busy wondering whether coincidence or *Qadar* was running my life to make a peep.

"I understand," Reem said, even though she understood as much about what was going on as I did about open-heart surgery. "And I appreciate you trying to protect us, Delilah."

Delilah waved her hand. "Bah! You're tough cookies. You don't need my protection anymore, even though I sometimes wish you did. Maybe that's why I called you yesterday, Reem. I got real worked up thinking about Asim being back, and overreacted when Scarlett told me she had a new case. I upset you for nothing, hon, and I'm sorry."

Reem smiled and squeezed Delilah's hand. "You don't have anything to apologize for. I don't know what I'd do if you and Mook weren't keeping an eye on Scarlett for me. Before you know it, though, I'll be done with my training, and Lettie will be off to college. She's going to do great things once we get her out of Las Almas. Just you wait and see."

"Oh," Delilah said, "I suspect our girl here will do

some pretty amazing stuff even before that. In fact, hard as it is for me to admit, something tells me she's right where she's supposed to be at the moment. Right where she's *meant* to be."

She looked at me, grave as an undertaker, then turned to Reem. "Each of you girls has a gift," she said. "You're a healer, Reem."

Her eyes came back to mine.

"And you, Scarlett? You're a warrior. It would be wrong for me or anyone else to try to hold you back. I see that now."

A warrior? Asim had called himself the same thing in our apartment.

Reem laughed. "I don't know if I'd go that far, Delilah. I'm only a resident, and Lettie's just nosy and stubborn."

Delilah's face lightened a bit. "You'd be surprised, sweetie," she said. "Besides, every girl needs to know that the people who love her believe in her, too. For the record, I believe in both of you. That's why I asked Reem to come see me, Scarlett—so I could apologize for making her worry so much about you. I know you're a good girl doing what you're meant to do, and I feel bad for not making peace with that sooner."

Reem stepped closer to Delilah and drew her into a hug of her own. "You're one of a kind, Delilah. Mom loved you, and so do we."

Delilah watched me over Reem's shoulder. Perky as she'd managed to sound, her eyes were filled with a sad kind of knowing.

"So I guess this means I should lay off you some, huh, Lettie?" Reem said as she let Delilah go.

"Nah." My voice sounded rough. "Where's the fun in that?"

Reem laughed. I was a better actor than I thought.

"In that case," Reem said, "I don't suppose you got the laundry done today, did you?"

I groaned and smacked my forehead.

"Big surprise," she said. "Good thing I keep a pair of underwear in reserve."

"I'll do it tomorrow," I promised.

Delilah smiled. "You two go home now, before it gets too late. I'm gonna lock up early once the General finishes his supper."

"Always happy to keep a lovely lady such as yourself company," the General called.

"Ears like a fox, that one has," Delilah said, tugging her shirt down over her waistband. "Now scoot."

She hustled us out of the diner, flipping the sign in the window from OPEN to CLOSED behind us.

Reem adjusted her *hijab* and shoved her hands in her pockets. "It got cold," she said.

"Sure did." I turned right without asking Reem which way she wanted to go. Left would have gotten us home just as fast, but by way of the Laundromat. And since I wasn't in a gambling mood, I didn't want to risk running into my tails.

"It's nice to be outside, especially with you here," Reem said.

I thought of Sam, of how deep and awful the hurt of missing his brother must be.

"Yeah," I said. "It is."

Other than the occasional metallic clang of shop gates closing and an echo of Cuban-tinted Spanish from the courtyard behind us, the street was quiet.

"And it'll be good, saying the *Isha* prayer together," Reem said. "When was the last time we got to start and end a day together?"

I took in a breath of cold air and looked past the lights of Las Almas, toward the stars they blotted out. Told her I couldn't remember. And then we walked the rest of the way home in silence, two sisters alone under a hidden sky.

14

Reem must have left for the hospital too early the next morning to rouse me for the *Fajr* prayer, because it was well past dawn when I woke. After I'd scalded myself in the shower, pulled on a mostly clean pair of jeans, and choked down a stale croissant, I snagged our dirty clothes and headed for the Laundromat. It was still cold out. My wrist hurt. My client wasn't safe from her own brother. And Deck hadn't responded to the text I'd sent the night before, asking how he could have forgotten to mention that his father was not only alive, but an asshole, to boot. Put that all together, and I was one grouchy ladybug, looking for a fight.

Turned out I didn't have to look very hard to find one.

I saw my tails before they saw me. Blondie was behind her paper in a new doorway; Shorty fiddled with her phone at one of the little tables outside Di-Santi's. Both were trying hard to look like they didn't have a care in the world. *Poor things*, I thought, *pining away for a glimpse of little old me.*

It wasn't enough to break your heart, but a few crocodile tears seemed in order.

I strolled toward the Laundromat, slow enough so there was no way they could miss me. Mook was on his stoop, lit cigarette burning its way toward his fingers. We hadn't spoken since he'd ticked me off the other day, before Calamus. I still couldn't figure how he'd known I was about to do something stupid. I still wished I didn't care.

"Howdy, Mook," I said.

"As-salaamu alaikum."

"All right, all right," I grumbled. *"Wa alaikum as-salaam."*

He dipped his head in a little nod. "That's better."

"I'm just checking in," I said. "Being so responsible and all."

His sloe-eyed stare stayed on the street. "And where are you going today?"

"To do laundry."

"And then?"

"City Hall. I've got a case to research while the washer runs."

A corner of his mouth crept up into a knowing half smile.

"This case you've taken on...it's a bit more than you expected, perhaps?"

Dammit, I thought. *He's doing it again.*

But all I said was, "Nah. Not so much."

The unsmiling half of his mouth twitched.

"It's not easy, you know, being your *mu'aqqibat*. And I have a feeling it's about to become more difficult."

"I never asked for a guardian angel, Mook. I don't even believe in them."

He ignored that. Took a drag and looked across the street toward DiSanti's.

"Have you spoken with Delilah lately?" he asked.

"Last night. At the Rubicon."

"She's a good soul, Delilah, and loyal. Sometimes to a fault."

"Sure," I said, doing my best to sidestep whatever

point he was working up to. "I guess I better get this stuff in a washer."

I started to push open the Laundromat door.

"*Akht?*"

I stopped.

"Yeah, Mook?"

"Watch your back."

"I always do."

He took another drag and blew the smoke out his nose. It was as close as he'd get to a good-bye.

I went inside. Loaded the machine. Went back out.

Mook was gone.

My tails were not.

As I moved down the street, the pair of them followed me tight. They weren't keen on being seen, but I'd already ditched them twice, and they didn't look ready to let it happen again. I crossed the street, waited until they'd done the same, then crossed back, just to mess with them.

Three blocks over, I turned into an alley and stepped behind a Dumpster. My blackjack was in my hand by the time Blondie caught up. She looked around, squinting toward the dead-end brick wall ahead.

"Ladies," I said, stepping out as Shorty joined us.

The gold in their eyes reminded me of toxic sludge. "How can I help you?"

Blondie let out something close to a snarl. Shorty looked insulted. Neither spoke.

"Not sure?" I said. "Then maybe you can tell me who you're working for and where you learned to do such a crap job running a tail."

"You little..." Shorty said. Blondie stopped her with a hand on the shoulder.

"You get one warning," Blondie said in a washed-out, reedy voice. "One. Go back to playing detective with your slum-rat neighbors and leave the real mysteries to us grown-ups."

"Is that all you were trying to do yesterday morning?" I said. "Offer me some friendly advice?"

Shorty didn't appreciate my rapier wit. In fact, it hacked her off so bad she came at me.

I dropped low, batted away her fumbling swing with a forearm block. Grabbed her collar with my left hand, hooked my right elbow, and swung up and inward to smash the spot where her jaw met her neck. She dropped like a sack of hot rocks. It shocked the hell out of Blondie; I knew it from the look on her face. And it didn't sit easy with me, either. Hurting people never did.

"Are you two part of the Children of Iblis?" I asked, tapping the blackjack against my palm to hide the shake in my hands. Blondie glanced at it nervously.

"*That* was a mistake," she said.

"Let's try again," I said. "Tell me what you know about the Children of Iblis."

Her lips curled back. Her eyes darted from the blackjack to Shorty, writhing on the ground.

"I'm not telling *you* anything," she spat.

Something in her voice, in the way she held her body, let me know I'd gotten to her. My shaking stopped.

"Then I guess we'll have to do things the hard way," I said. "Because I'm real good at my job, and real bad at letting things go. Sooner or later, I'll bust up your little freak show. And when that happens, I guarantee you're not gonna like it."

Her laugh was like metal scraping metal. "You'll be dead soon, you know."

"We'll all be dead soon, lady."

She shook her head. "You have no idea, do you?"

"Not usually, no."

The gold in her eyes hardened.

"There *is* no death for us, little detective. Once the ring is ours, we'll live forever."

"Sure. You go with that," I said, and walked out of the alley without a backward glance. She didn't follow me, but at the next intersection, I could have sworn I caught a flash of Mook's duster, turning past a building to my left.

"Mook?" I called out.

But there was no response, no sign of Mook when I rounded the corner.

Two against one and a death threat on top of that, I thought. *And my guardian angel just walks away.*

The downtown bus I needed pulled into its stop a few blocks up. Even if I ran, I wouldn't catch it.

"Dumb freakin' luck," I said to no one in particular. And started to walk.

The doors to City Hall were still locked when I got there, which left me standing out in the morning wind for ten minutes, cursing Las Almas bureaucrats for not waking up early like the rest of the world. I was cold, I was impatient, and I needed more info on The Parker and George Fagin. That meant digging through the hellish stacks of permits, blueprints, and assorted useless documents they kept on file in the records office.

It was slow, tedious, old-school detective work. And in a twisted sort of way, I liked it.

City Hall was a stoic building, impressive and grand and as stuffy as they came. Back before the stock market crash in the twenties, when millionaires did their best to prove new money could buy class, a bunch of old white guys had built the place and passed it on to future generations of old white guys. I always wore my secondhand biker boots there because they felt so inappropriate. Today, I'd brought along my dark gray fedora to class the joint up even more.

"Hey, Delores. How's it going?" I said at the records office window. Delores and I went way back. The first time I'd visited, she'd ignored me. When I rang the desk bell in front of her, she'd ignored me even harder. It had not been an auspicious start.

"Whaddaya want?"

Her cherry menthol breath hit my nose. Delores never said hello, never smiled, and always had a lozenge in her yap. She was a sour woman with a perpetual sore throat and an appliquéd sweater for every occasion.

"Permits and blueprints for The Parker, please."

"Copies? Or you just gonna look?"

"Copies, please."

"Got cash?"

"Always."

"Requisition slip?"

I handed her the form, filled out in my neatest print.

"Take a seat," she said.

"Thanks, Delores. You're a pal."

She grunted. I sat in a molded plastic chair and tried not to dwell on how uncomfortable it was. Things in the records office moved slower than glaciers, so the best thing to do was make peace with the awful decor and ponder the string of teddy bears marching across Delores's doughy bosom.

Forty-five minutes later she called me to her window.

"There's nothing there," she said.

"Come again?"

"There's. Nothing. There. Whole file's gone."

"Everything? Every single one of The Parker's records?"

She gave me a look like salted lemons.

"How could that happen?" I said. "Those files aren't supposed to leave the archive."

"Brass probably took 'em out." She shrugged. "They can do that."

"Could the file have been stolen?"

She shrugged again.

"Aren't there duplicates?"

The brown lines penciled in where her eyebrows should have been crept higher on her forehead.

"And it took you forty-five minutes to tell me this?" I said.

Delores smiled and hollered, "Next!"

"Delores?"

The brown lines lifted again.

"You're a real pip."

"Have a nice day," she said. "Come again soon."

I stomped out of the records office and back across the rotunda, loud enough to make the decrepit old security guard frown. He didn't like it when I asked for my black-jack back, either, but then, I hadn't liked giving it to him in the first place. "Thanks for guarding Thumper," I said.

He pointed a gnarled finger at me, scrunched his eyebrows low, and was just about to learn me but good when my phone rang. "Gotta go," I said, and scooted outside to answer the call.

"Hello?" The voice on the other end of the line was Gemma's. She didn't sound good.

"Where are you, kid?"

"In the janitor's closet at school," she said in something just north of a whisper.

I sank down onto the steps, sick at myself for not checking in with her earlier that morning. "What's going on? Are you all right?"

"For now. But Oliver just came to my class and tried to get Mrs. Thomas to let me leave with him. He said he needed to tell me something personal. If we hadn't been in the middle of a math test, she'd have let me go. She sent me to the main office after I finished. I came here instead."

"That was smart, Gemma," I said. "Really smart."

"I think he was going to take me."

"Take you where?"

"Nowhere good."

I remembered the text Quinn never saw on his phone— the one threatening Sam—and knew she was right.

"Listen, Gemma, I need you to go to the nurse's office and tell them you just threw up."

"Okay." Her voice was tiny.

"You give the nurse my number and say I'm supposed to come get you, that I'm your new nanny."

"There's a pickup list," she said. "If you're not on it, they won't let me go with you."

I stood up and started toward the street.

"All right," I said. "Then scratch that plan and just

stay put. I'll be there in ten minutes. Don't move. Is there a security guard at the door?"

"No. Stokes walks around the halls. There's a buzzer to the office by the front gate that you have to ring for them to let you in."

"Fine. I'll call you when I'm outside. Then you go to the office and tell them you've been sick, that you called your nanny from the bathroom because you were scared. I'll hit the buzzer up front, and you ID me on the security camera. That should get me inside. I'll take it from there."

She sniffled.

"Can you do that for me, Gemma?"

"Uh-huh."

"Good. You hang tight, kid, and call me if anything happens. I'm coming for you."

"Okay," she said. "But, Scarlett?"

"Yeah?" I said, racing a slick-haired, pin-striped lawyer-type to the lone cab parked on the curb. My hat flew off. I didn't look back.

"Please hurry."

"I'm coming, kid," I said, getting into the cab. The suit flipped me off from ten feet back.

"Just hang on."

15

For my first visit to Chandler Academy, I'd dressed in a blue pleated skirt, joined the crush of bodies pouring in ahead of the first bell, planted my business cards in the bathrooms, and walked right back out. No muss, no fuss. And thanks to the story I'd cooked up with Gemma, getting in the second time around was cake, too.

Smuggling her out was a different matter altogether.

I found her in the office, looking miserable. As soon as she saw me, she ran over and threw herself into my arms.

Again with the affection, I thought, smiling in spite of myself.

"You're the Archers' new nanny?" the secretary asked. According to the nameplate on the desk, her first name was Miss, her last was Pritchard. Cat's-eye glasses hung from a chain around her neck, and the hairs in her bun were yanked so tight I could hear their follicles weep.

"I am," I said in my best "yes ma'am" voice. "Gemma called to say she's been sick."

"So she tells me." Pritchard gave my biker boots a hard look. "Nurse McMahon is on his way down."

She'd barely finished saying so when a man walked in wearing freckled forearms that would have put Popeye's to shame.

"Well?" He whipped a thermometer out of the pocket of his skull-and-crossbones scrubs. Waggled it at us. "Which one of you just had the reverse breakfast?"

"Miss Archer was ill," the secretary said with a curt nod toward Gemma.

The nurse gave Gemma a wink, swiped the thermometer across her forehead, and checked the readout.

"No fever," he said, cupping her cheek in his catcher's mitt of a hand. "But you're clammy and you look like a bleached sheet. How'd you feel when you left the house this morning?"

"A little funny, I guess."

"Anyone else in your family sick?"

"My cousin threw up yesterday. I've been helping take care of him."

Good job, kid, I thought.

"Then, Miss Pritchard," McMahon said, "in my highly trained medical opinion, this young lady has a bad case of the cooties and should go home."

Miss Pritchard settled her glasses onto the bridge of her nose. "Very well, then. I'll have to contact her parents...."

"They're at work," Gemma said. "Scarlett's supposed to get me if I'm sick."

"She's not on the list." Miss Pritchard gave me a look like I'd let her down.

McMahon sighed. "Honestly, Victoria, there's some kind of nasty stomach bug making the rounds right now. The sooner we get Gemma home the better. I don't want this thing wiping out the whole school."

Pritchard pulled something up on her computer and jabbed at the phone keys like they'd insulted her mother. Air whistled through her narrow nostrils. After a while, she hung up and tried again. Gemma looked over at me, eyes huge. I smiled and tried to coax my own pulse back below heart-attack range.

If either of the Archers picked up, things could get hairy.

"Neither parent answers," Pritchard said.

I snuck a relieved breath.

She hung up, frowned, pounded something new into the keyboard, and picked up the phone to dial again. That time, only three keys felt her wrath.

"Mr. Klein? I believe you have Oliver Archer there in class with you?" She scratched at something on the computer screen with her nail. "Very good. Would you send him down to the office, please? Thank you."

McMahon gave me a sympathetic wink. Gemma looked ready to crawl under a chair.

"I'm sorry to seem so inflexible," Miss Pritchard said, "but nothing is more important than student safety here at Chandler Academy. Once Miss Archer's brother confirms that you're employed by his family, I'll be able to let you take her home. I hope you understand."

I knew she didn't give a monkey's behind whether I understood a thing, but I smiled anyway and made nice.

"I'll just head back to the infirmary, then." McMahon gave Gemma's arm a tender little squeeze. "Holler if you need anything else."

Pritchard smiled vaguely and looked through him into the hallway. "Very good," she said. "Here's Mr. Archer now."

If Gemma had been pale before, the sight of her brother made her go all but translucent. Her chest rose and fell like a hummingbird's. I stepped closer and took her hand.

"How can I help you, Miss Pritchard?" Oliver sounded like a bad used-car salesman, and Pritchard was in a buying mood.

"Well, Mr. Archer, it seems your sister is ill and needs to be escorted home. If you could just confirm that this young woman is, in fact, Gemma's nanny, then you may go back to class."

Oliver pivoted toward us.

"What's the matter, sis?" His voice was sickly sweet.

"I threw up," Gemma said softly.

My own voice was strong.

"I should get her home, Oliver. Your parents have too much on their minds as it is. I'd hate to have to bother them with all . . . *this*."

I could see his anger, see him thinking through different ways this scene could play out. The last thing he wanted was for his parents to find out about the Children of Iblis, or about his involvement with Quinn

Johnson's death. For now, at least, our little game of cat and mouse was rigged, and not in his favor.

"You looked fine this morning, sis," he said through a rigid jaw. "What happened?"

Gemma's chin trembled. "I just don't feel good, Oliver. Please let Scarlett take me home."

Oliver's eyes narrowed down to ugly slits. I squeezed Gemma's hand tighter.

"This *is* your sister's nanny, then, Mr. Archer?" Pritchard had clearly had enough of the Archer family's traveling road show for one morning.

I looked from Oliver's eyes to his wrist and back again, letting him know I'd force my hand if I had to. Pritchard cleared her throat.

"Mr. Archer?"

"She"—he spat the words out point first—"works for our family."

Pritchard nodded. "Thank you. That will be all, Mr. Archer."

She could have been talking to the wall for all Oliver cared.

"I know you'll feel better with Scarlett taking care of you, sis," he said, resting his hand on Gemma's shoulder as he passed. "But I'll check in on you. Soon."

I pulled her toward me. "Don't worry, Oliver. I'm not about to let anything happen to your sister."

He gave me a look hard enough to cut diamonds, and stalked out.

"Thank you, Miss Pritchard," I said after the office door had slammed shut behind him. "I appreciate everything you do to keep Gemma safe."

The secretary's lips twitched. Either she was immune to my charms, or I was losing my touch.

Must have been immunity.

"Do notify me if Miss Archer is still ill tomorrow morning," Pritchard said stiffly.

I pulled Gemma even closer. "Miss Pritchard," I said, hustling Gemma out, "I'll be sure to do that."

By the time Gemma was tucked in safe and sound at her aunt's, I had just enough time to get to the ass-end of Las Almas before the clock hit one. The other night, I'd threatened Asim with not going to Calamus, but he and I had both known it was a bluff. And a bad one, at that.

"Third and Doyle," I told the cab driver. He had a

white beard and a tweed hat and his cab smelled like Lysol. I had no problem with Lysol. Especially in cabs.

"You sure about that?" He looked at me in his rear-view, dubious.

"Unfortunately, I am," I said, pulling out my phone. There was a message from Deck waiting.

Working early tomorrow. Stop by?

I ignored it. Not hearing from him the night before had sat about as well as bad sushi. He must have known Delilah was going to drop the Asim-is-Decker's-dad thing on me like two tons of bricks, and as much as my heart wanted me to talk to him, my head wanted him to suffer. So I texted Gemma instead.

Stay put! And tell me when your aunt gets home from work.

A smiley face with a stuck-out tongue came back fast. I sent her one with a wink. Then I contemplated checking in with Reem, decided it would be overkill. Turning into a good girl overnight would set off my sister's BS detector and very possibly wreck the freedom Delilah's little performance at the Rubicon had bought me.

"You *really* sure?" the driver said as the buildings started going postapocalyptic.

"Yep," I said. "And by the way, thanks for coming

out this far. A lot of guys would have dumped me off four blocks back."

He tipped his hat and smiled. "That's my job. You pay, I drive."

I thought about how that would look on my business card. *Scarlett: You pay, I snoop.* It had a nice ring to it. Hopefully things really would be that simple after I put this case to bed, and I could go back to tracking down stray boyfriends and runaways.

Hopefully I wasn't hoping for too much.

"Here's fine," I told the driver when Third ran into Doyle. Compared to the last time I'd visited, the place was hopping. Two drug slingers were shooting dice on a stoop five doors down from Calamus. The one-eyed dog was there, too. She sat, still as a statue, watching my cab roll to a stop. Across the street, an old woman with a grocery cart waved her arms and shook her fist at the sky, arguing with someone nobody else could see. And, of course, there was the creep in the doorway, still covered from head to toe in filthy rags, still swaying.

"You know them?" the driver asked. I could tell he didn't like the look of the corner boys, but they were the least of my worries.

"I'll be fine. Thanks." I paid my fare plus a big tip

and stood on the curb until he was gone. The stoop boys looked me over. They were interested. I slipped my blackjack out of my bag, tapped it against my thigh. They went back to their dice. Turned out they weren't so interested after all.

Next, I walked up to the swaying creep and looked him straight in the spot where his eyes must have been.

"Afternoon," I said.

He stopped swaying. Didn't hiss. Didn't move.

"So," I said, "I was hoping you could explain exactly to whom or what you were referring the other night. That I should stay away from, I mean."

There was no movement, but I felt his energy shift. A gloved hand reached up abruptly and bumped the scarf just far enough to expose a pair of gold-ringed green eyes.

"Oh, for hell's sake!"

The scarf came down completely. The hat came off. And he wasn't a he.

He was a she.

Quick as a fourth-grade kiss, the woman grabbed my wrist and pulled me toward Calamus, muttering so quickly and quietly I could only catch snippets like, "no bloody fear," "no respect," and "dreadful country." She dragged me up the church's old stone steps, through the front door, past the beaded doorway, and into the sanctuary. Just inside sat an odd assortment of mismatched chairs, metal cabinets, and a wheeled stainless steel table holding a tattoo gun. An enormous Persian carpet covered the stone floor. The rest of the space was pure church.

"Stay here," she said. "Don't move." She disappeared behind the chancel, leaving me face-to-face with a statue of a mournful Virgin Mary cradling Jesus's crumpled body. *Enough with the dead sons, already*, I thought, and looked around for something cheerier.

Four stained glass windows stretched across the back wall of the building, safe from street-side vandals. My mother had been a devout Muslim who hated ignorance as much as sin. She'd dragged Reem and me to all kinds of temples and churches, telling us we needed to understand other faiths to appreciate our own. So I knew all about the apostles and saints going about their business in the glass. But the far-left pane was what really caught my eye. It showed a naked Eve with long, conveniently arranged red hair, offering an apple to Adam. Adam looked dull and hungry.

Eventually, the tattoo guy came out from behind the chancel.

"*As-salaamu alaikum*," I said.

"*Wa alaikum as-salaam.*" He offered me his hand, which was a surprise. A lot of Muslim men wouldn't do that for a woman. I slipped off the blackjack strap and shook his hand. His grip was firm. Mine was, too.

"So," I said, "how about that tattoo?"

He studied me with bottomless eyes, then laughed, loud and full.

"Come with me, child. And welcome to my home."

He didn't have to ask twice.

16

I followed Manny behind the chancel and down a narrow spiral staircase. The smell of spices and meat hit me, as unexpected in the musty old church as jugglers at a funeral. At the bottom we walked through a plain wooden door that opened like Alice's looking glass into a room spanning the whole basement of the church. Clusters of furniture and folding screens divided the place into living areas decorated like something out of a design magazine. All four walls were lined with floor-to-ceiling bookshelves. Platters of lamb, spiced green beans, vermicelli rice, tabbouleh, hummus, pita, and chocolate-covered dates were laid out on a long wooden table next to the kitchen. It was more food than I'd seen in one place since *Ummi* died. Three places were set.

"You shouldn't have," I said. "Especially since I didn't know you were going to."

Manny motioned for me to sit. "I apologize for the abrupt nature of your invitation. Asim possesses a number of remarkable qualities, but tact has never numbered among them."

The meal thing had me off my game. Food was for guests. *Ummi* had raised me knowing that guests were to be fed, honored, then fed some more. They were supposed to bring a gift, too.

"I'd have brought something if I'd known," I said.

"You came. That is enough." Manny bowed his head.

"You didn't seem to think so the other day," I said.

"I didn't expect you the other day. Perhaps this afternoon we'll both be more...in tune with each other." He smiled.

A drawer slammed shut at the back of the room and the rag lady stepped out from behind a four-panel silk screen. Only she wasn't in rags anymore.

From the halo of raven-black hair pinned up with silver combs to the slender arms and legs peeking out from her silver-embroidered kimono, everything about her was gorgeous. Her smooth skin shone against the apartment's rich fabrics; her seashell-pink nails matched the natural blush on her high cheekbones.

You could have knocked me over with a sneeze.

Then one of her toes caught on the curved leg of a chair, and she let loose a banshee shriek.

"Shite!" She dropped into the chair. Yanked her foot up to inspect the damage. "You and all this abominable, heavy furniture!" she raged. "There are only two of us! Why in Hades do we have so many chairs?"

"Nuala, dear," Manny said calmly, "we should eat."

"I'll be lucky if the fekkin' nail doesn't come off!" she groused.

"Scarlett, you'll have to forgive my wife." Manny got up to pull out her chair. "I'm afraid she takes the hot-tempered Irish stereotype rather seriously."

That earned him a dirty look and a string of curses from Nuala that would have made the drug slingers out front blush. It was just the kick in the crotch I needed to help me remember this wasn't a social call. I was there on business.

"Look," I said, "I appreciate dinner and a date as

much as the next girl, but that's not why I accepted your invitation. I came because I think you might be able to help me bail out a grade-schooler who's in trouble up to her eyeballs, and because your pal Asim stole something from me that he can't keep. So if you don't mind, let's skip the formalities and start talking for real."

Manny looked wounded. Nuala cracked a Cheshire grin and chuckled. "You've got a bloody cheek on you, girl!"

For just a second, Manny's expression was enough to make the guilty little Muslim kid inside me duke it out with the pushy detective. The detective won.

"Give me back my bottle, answer a few questions, and I'll get out of your hair and let you get back to"— I looked around the room, at the mismatched pair of them—"whatever it is you do."

"Ask what you will," Manny said. Nuala settled in, ready for the show to start.

I put everything on the table at once, no punches pulled.

"Who are you, what do you know about my father, and what can you tell me about the *Shubaak*, King Solomon's ring, and the Children of Iblis?"

Manny shook his head. "So sure of yourself," he said quietly. "So sure and so impatient."

I pushed my chair back and stood up. "Where's my *abbi*'s bottle?"

He sighed. Closed his eyes. "Please," he said, opening them slowly. "Sit."

I did, but hard enough to let him know I wasn't happy about it.

"Are you sure you want to hear?" he asked.

I didn't answer, just glared.

"Very well, then."

He gave Nuala a nervous glance. She arched a cryptic eyebrow. He started talking.

"I'll begin with the ring. As the legends say, it was a powerful seal that gave Solomon dominion over weather and beasts. Humankind and jinnkind, as well."

"What about his seven hundred wives and three hundred concubines?" Nuala snarked. "What effect did the ring have on them?"

Manny smiled patiently, but his eyes gave nothing away.

"To continue," he said, "the ring was given to Solomon by Nathan the Prophet as Solomon's father, King David, lay dying. It was adorned with an interlocking design that resembled the one you saw on the door of your young friend's brother, and on Decker's chest, as well."

He paused, making sure I'd kept up. I had.

"Solomon was intelligent and respected the inner spark—the divinity—in every living creature. The ring magnified those qualities."

"Sure. Right up until he died and it disappeared," I said, thinking back to Dr. Sawalha's article about the *Shubaak*.

Manny suddenly looked tired.

"The ring did not disappear. It was taken, along with the *Shubaak*, by Solomon's most beloved wife, known to us only as Pharaoh's daughter. She entrusted the ring to her firstborn son, and the *Shubaak* to her second-born—a daughter. Both were charged with the safekeeping of those objects, and both made a covenant to pass that duty on to their heirs."

"And you know this because . . . ?" I said.

"I know this because *I* am an heir of Solomon. *I* broke the family covenant. *I* grew careless and began wearing the ring openly."

He paused. Took a jagged breath.

"Forty-three years ago a pickpocket stole the ring

from my finger on a crowded Las Almas street. And I would very much like it back."

❈

Nuala handed Manny a goblet of water. Manny gulped it down like he'd just come in from the desert. "Dearest," Nuala said, "we've discussed this so many times. You have to forgive yourself in order for us to move on and recover the ring."

Manny sighed. "You're right, my love." He reached for the pitcher, filled the glass up again.

"So your name," I said, feeling a little bad for the guy. "Manny. Short for Suleyman. Solomon. I get it."

"Clever girl," Manny said. "What else have you deduced?"

"Enough to keep me going, not enough to brag about. One thing that's driving me nuts is what makes the ring and the *Shubaak* worth dying over. Are they really that special?"

Nuala snuck a sideways glance at Manny.

"I suppose that depends on who you talk to," he said.

"Well, at the moment, I'm talking to you. What do *you* think?"

Manny rested his forearms on the table. "I'd like you to tell me what you know of jinn."

I shrugged. "The basics, I guess. Allah made them from smokeless fire, like he made angels from light and humans from clay. That's what the Quran says, at least."

"Exactly." Manny set his glass down. "In Islamic theology, jinn live and die in a realm beyond human perception and are rarely, if ever, seen by us. But according to some accounts—call them myths or folklore—jinn were once able to travel between our worlds through portals, called *Shubaak*. Just like humans, jinn could be good, bad, or somewhere in between. The problem was, their ability to manipulate the laws of physics in this realm made them extremely powerful. Immortal, even. Thanks to his ring, Solomon managed to control that power and maintain a fragile peace for many years. Right up until Iblis declared war against humankind."

"The Children of Iblis," I whispered.

"That's right," Manny said. "As I'm sure you know, Iblis was the jinn who refused Allah's command to bow down before Adam, peace be upon him. Iblis believed mankind was inferior to the jinn, having been created later, and from clay rather than fire. After he fell from grace with Allah, Iblis convinced other weak-minded and wicked jinn to join with him in his war. Together, they were called the Children of Iblis, and they grew extremely influential during Solomon's reign. In fact, were it not for Solomon's ability to hold them in check, humans would have been enslaved by jinn thousands of years ago. And slaves we would still be today."

"Okay, so where does the *Shubaak* come in?" I asked, thinking back to Dr. Sawalha's paper.

"We'll get to that momentarily," Manny said. "For as Solomon grew older, Iblis and his followers devised a plan to steal the ring. A small group of jinn loyal to Solomon learned of Iblis's plan, and told their king. It was then that Solomon realized no human would ever be truly safe as long as jinn were allowed to remain in this realm, practicing what amounted to magic. So he issued a decree that all jinn were to return to their own world by sunrise the next day, or remain trapped here, stripped of their powers and immortality, forever."

I dropped my chin into my hands. "The ring let him turn them into humans?"

"Effectively, yes. Now, at that time, there were four *Shubaak*, four portals to the jinn realm, in existence. When sunrise came, Solomon destroyed three of them, saving the last for fear of destroying completely a passage willed by Allah. Then he used the ring's magic to strip all powers from those jinn who had ignored his warning, trapping them on this side forever. And where their eyes had once been the color of pure gold, Solomon took all but the trace of it you see around the irises of the jinn's descendants today."

I looked at Nuala. "You have those eyes. So do Asim and Decker and the two women following me around town like bad credit."

"Of course they do," Manny said. "They are descended from the Children of Iblis. Some, like Asim and Nuala, wear the reminder of their ancestor's rebellion like a scar. Others consider it a call to arms, and believe that finding Solomon's ring will restore their rightful powers. The Children of Iblis have convinced their followers that if they gain possession of the ring and the *Shubaak* King Solomon chose not to destroy, they will be able to reopen the passage between human and jinn realms, and bring forth jinn armies to enslave humanity. In short, to the Children of Iblis, the rebellion that began three thousand years ago is still very much alive."

"So," I said, putting my doubts on hold, "there are

167

certain genetically linked...*individuals* with gold-ringed eyes running around Las Almas, calling themselves the Children of Iblis, looking for a ring and a bottle they think will give them magical powers and let them take over the world."

Manny nodded.

"And magical or not, any artifact from King Solomon's reign definitely would be worth a fortune and a half," I went on. "Add in the fact that these *individuals* believe they're actually jinn, and that makes them dangerous for real."

"Precisely," Manny said. "They are very, very dangerous."

All the things I'd learned from Sam and Emmet were starting to fit together like double-sided puzzle pieces. There really was a cult out there—a cult of batshit crazy, funky-eyed nut jobs convinced they were genies poised to take over the world. To make things worse, they were brainwashing high school kids, getting them to help hunt down Solomon's ring and the *Shubaak* and do God knew what else. Gemma had been right: her brother was in trouble. Serious, messed-up trouble.

I pressed the inside corners of my eyes. Took a deep breath.

"So Asim's like them, only he's on our side?"

Manny was watching me gravely. "Correct."

"And Decker's his son."

"Yes."

"Asim said he knew my *abbi*." I spoke carefully, taking care not to mince a single word. "How?"

"Your *abbi* was a descendant of King Solomon and Pharaoh's daughter. That made him an *Abd al-Malik*. A Servant of the King, like me."

My hand went to my backpack. *One Thousand and One Nights* was inside, *Abd al-Malik* inscription and all. Even under a layer of nylon, the physical reminder of my father was a comfort.

"Then you and *Abbi* are related?" I asked.

"Distantly. As are you and I. But where my family line traces its roots to Solomon's son, yours and your father's goes back to his daughter."

"And *Abbi* was guarding the *Shubaak*, just like Solomon's daughter?"

Manny gave me a tired smile. "The *Shubaak* and two of the three decoys created by King Solomon to replace those destroyed and confound the Children of Iblis. And now that you know all of this, it falls to you to assume your family's duty."

"Come again?"

"You were your father's chosen, Scarlett. He knew you were the new *Abd al-Malik* from the moment you entered the world, silent as dawn, with your eyes wide open. You have never shied away from life, my dear. Your sister is the healer. You are the warrior."

"Did you tell Delilah I'm this *Abd al-Malik* thing so she'd get off my back last night?" I was flailing, trying to find some kind of toehold against the avalanche coming down on me.

"She has always known. I only reminded her."

"Well, thanks for that, I guess."

"You're welcome."

He was so earnest I almost smiled. Then I remembered Asim and didn't. "You know the *Shubaak* Asim stole from me is a fake, right?" I said.

Manny's face fell. He stood up, walked to a desk against the wall, and pulled the bottle from our curio cabinet out of a bottom drawer. "I suspected as much, but had hoped to be wrong." He sat back down and handed it to me. "You're positive this is not the true *Shubaak*?"

"*Abbi* told us it was just an old souvenir," I said. "He kept it out in the open in our apartment."

"Then it could not possibly be," Manny said.

"So you're telling me bottles weren't genie prisons like in the stories?"

"The stories are wrong on that count. *Shubaak* were, as I have said, portals."

I rubbed my thumb across the bottle's lid. A lot of Manny's story was still sinking in.

He leaned toward me.

"Scarlett?"

"Hmm?"

"I'm quite certain the Children of Iblis killed your *abbi* in the process of stealing what they believed to be the real *Shubaak*."

Nuala shifted in her seat. It was all I could do to breathe.

"Scarlett?"

I didn't move.

"Was the real *Shubaak* with him the night he died?" Manny asked. "Or was it a decoy?"

We were heading down a path I'd never even known was there. It was too much. Too fast. Too everything.

And then, suddenly, it wasn't. Time slowed, and my mind cleared.

"You know," I said, the lie slipping off my tongue like truth. "I haven't got a clue."

17

Walking home from Calamus was a terrible idea, so that was exactly what I did. The stoop boys outside the church made kissing sounds and rude suggestions as I passed by. The dog trotted behind me. I didn't care. I knew why my father was dead.

The cancer that stole *Ummi* was easy to understand, easy to hate. But zealots had killed *Abbi*, and that was different. Hating them came easy as breathing. Understanding them was a whole lot tougher. And the more I thought about it, the less I *wanted* to understand. Maybe blame had been the anchor I'd needed all these years. With someone to go after, I wouldn't have to forget. Or forgive.

Halfway home, the dog was still behind me.

"Beat it," I said.

She sat, letting me build enough of a lead to think she'd listened. Next thing I knew, she was back again.

"Seriously?"

She cocked her head. Scratched her belly with a back paw.

"Whatever."

She yawned.

I turned and started walking again, going over everything Manny had said. On one level, it all made sense. Stolen antiques, cults, crazies loose on the streets of Las Almas—those were the kinds of things private detectives *got*. Dreamed of, even. But genies and magic rings? They might have been fun to read about, or watch onscreen in a dark movie theater, but you didn't let them into real life. You didn't *believe* in them.

The wind took on an ugly bite. I pulled my jacket tighter, walked faster. The closer I got to my neighborhood, the more the sidewalks filled up with people. Compared with Third and Doyle, this was a living, breathing place. The hum of it all flushed out some of my chill. It was good. It just wasn't enough.

I needed Decker.

So I headed to the Rubicon. Found it dark inside and locked up tight behind its metal security grate.

Monday. Dammit.

Delilah never opened the place on Mondays. Sometimes Deck came in to take deliveries and get a jump on prep work, though. *Please be here*, I pleaded silently, heading down the building's side alley. *Please, please, please.*

Latches clicked. The back door swung open while I was still pounding on it. And there stood Decker, looking all kinds of wonderful.

"I was hoping you'd show," he said. "C'mon in."

The kitchen was warm and damp and smelled like home.

"Stock for matzo ball soup." He motioned toward a pot big enough to stew a whole flock of chickens.

I fell into him, wrapped my arms around him, and held tight.

"Hey...." His body tensed, then softened and closed around me. I felt his breath against my skin. Pressed my cheek into the curve where his neck met his shoulder.

His pulse steadied mine. Slowly, the blood in my veins defrosted and started to flow.

We stayed there, not moving, not speaking, pots simmering around us. It was perfect. I'd needed perfect.

"Who are you?" I whispered.

"You know the answer to that," Decker murmured into my hair.

I pulled away, hating myself for it, and watched the gold flecks around his irises dance in the steam.

"You know what I mean," I said.

"Yeah." He sighed. "You want to sit down?"

"Yeah."

We pushed through the swinging door to the dining room. I hopped onto one of the counter stools. Deck pointed to a half-full pot of coffee on the burner.

"Want some?"

"I'm good," I said. "Let's just talk."

He nodded, ran his hands through dark hair cut too short for his curls to show. "How'd things go at Calamus?"

"You knew I was there?"

He shrugged. Looked guilty.

"Scarlett..."

The look in my eyes must have made him stop.

"You should have told me what was going on, Deck," I said quietly.

"I couldn't. I wasn't supposed to."

"What do you mean you weren't *supposed* to? Since when do you take orders from anyone?"

"It's not like that," he said. "I wasn't following orders—I was trying to do things the way they're meant to be done. This is all bigger than you and me, Scarlett."

"No, it's not. It's just fairy tales and delusions."

He shook his head. "It's definitely more than that."

"A magic ring and an old bottle that's really a door to genie land? Are you kidding me?"

Deck frowned and shook his head. "Solomon's ring and the *Shubaak* aren't fairy tales. They're our history, Scarlett. Where we come from. And that's worth saving."

"Okay," I said, "but even if that's true, from what Manny told me, the Children of Iblis are doing this because they actually believe all the magic stuff. And I got the feeling he believes it, too. I mean, the guy's all torn up about losing the ring. He thinks he's an *Abd al-Malik*."

Deck looked sheepish. It suited him.

"What about Delilah?" I asked. "Does she believe?"

"A little, maybe. But she's not all weird about it. It's more like she figures there's no harm believing, just in case it's true. Because if it is, and if the Children of Iblis find the ring and the *Shubaak*, we're all sunk."

"What about you?"

"I don't know yet. I'm still sorting things out," Deck said. "When both of your parents believe in something, when it's what they expect *you* to believe, it's kind of hard not to at least give it a good think. And you're going to have to do the same, Scarlett. Your parents believed, too."

He rested his knee against mine. I thought about pulling back. Didn't.

"You told me your father was dead," I said.

"Up until last year, I thought he was." Decker tucked a strand of curls behind my ear. I tried to brush his hand away, but he caught my wrist right where it was tender, and hard enough to make me wince.

"I'm sorry!" Deck jerked his hand away, looking ready to throw himself on a sword. "Did I hurt you?"

"Not you. Asim." I tugged up my sleeve so he could see. He ran the tips of his fingers over the swelling, gentle as a butterfly kiss.

"He knocked me down, shoving his way into our apartment Saturday night," I said. "I landed funny."

Deck's face went grim. "He shouldn't have done that."

"No shit."

"I'll talk to him."

I pulled my hand away. "Don't bother. From what I can tell, he's way too into this mess to see things rationally."

Deck tried to turn his head away, but I put my hand on his cheek and brought it back.

"Even if you aren't sure about the magic part, Deck, do you believe your ancestors were jinn?"

He looked at me then like there was nothing between us, nothing to mark where I ended and he began.

"I don't know."

The raw honesty of his answer filled up a deep, empty spot inside me that I hadn't known was there. I came off my stool and moved to him. Pressed my hands against his chest. Felt the warmth of him through his cotton T-shirt. My hands slid to his waist. Around. Up the muscles of his back.

He didn't move. I kissed him.

It was warm and sweet and walking off a cliff, all at once. My tongue traced the curve of his upper lip.

He held back, letting me. Then it was too much and he pressed me to him hard. His tongue licked at mine. His free hand slipped to the small of my back, electric with want and promise.

And then he pulled away.

"No," he said. "Not like this."

"What do you mean?" My breath came fast. "I thought this was what you wanted."

His fingers slid from the top of my spine to wander over my lips. "You know it is."

"Then what?" I pulled his hand away, held it as I bumped back against my stool. "What's wrong?"

"It...it's just the timing, I guess," he said. "This shouldn't happen when everything's so screwed up. I mean, you just found out about your family. Things must be so surreal for you right now. You need time to make sense of it all without having to think about us. Because I know that *we're* real. You and me. We're real, and that's never going to change."

I played with the hairs on his wrist.

"Okay," I said.

His lips brushed my cheek. And then we sat there, hands touching, listening to the wall clock count out minutes.

179

"Scarlett?"

I looked up.

"I…" He paused, exhaled, tried again until I stopped him.

"I know, Deck. Me too."

He nodded. "Yeah."

And that was all we needed to say.

⊗

I left the Rubicon alone, even though Deck had offered to go with me. Insisted, even. But I turned him down. Needing him was one thing. Needing him to protect me was another.

The smell of chicken stock seeped out of my cardigan and into my nose as I walked, reminding me that no matter how Deck made me feel, a girl can't live on stomach butterflies alone. So I swung by the Vietnamese place around the corner from our apartment and picked up two orders of pho. Reem's went into the fridge; mine went into bed with me.

Everything was easier to take once the pillows at my back were arranged just so. It freed up my mind, let me focus on the questions that still needed answering. Like why the Children of Iblis were after George Fagin. And what had been on the paper shreds Quinn threw off the bridge before he jumped.

I sipped my broth and was about to shovel in a mouthful of noodles when a strange chime sounded in my backpack.

It was Quinn's phone. Had to be.

I shoved the container aside, pawed through the backpack and came up with the phone. A push notification lit the screen.

SoldierofIblis34 said: Traitor

I hit the icon next to the message, and a photo sharing account for SoldierofIblis21 came up. Even though I'd never seen the boy in the picture before, his round cheeks, freckles, and bushy red hair were so much like Sam's it spooked me. SoldierofIblis21 was Quinn Johnson.

They said they'll hurt my little brother if I
don't give them Fagin.
I waited too long.
Get out while you can.

Quinn had posted the picture and its caption the day he died. Since then, a string of comments had piled up underneath.

SoldierofIblis14 said: Seriously dude?

SoldierofIblis30 said: U r an idiot

SoldierofIblis5 said: Rot in hell asswipe

And on and on.

Some detective you are, Scarlett, I thought. *Any shamus worth her salt and pepper should be able to search a phone right, especially when it comes straight from a dead boy's hand.*

I'd just flunked Gumshoe 101.

It wouldn't happen again.

A quick look at Quinn's followers gave me a list of SoldierofIblis usernames, numbered one through thirty-six, along with one more that stuck out like a sore, festering thumb: IBLIS.

I tapped the screen, closed my eyes as Iblis's photos loaded. When I opened them, a single picture was onscreen, showing the Baker Street Bridge and a caption from that morning.

Soi1 and Soi2

1:00 pm Tuesday

That was when I knew that even though I'd screwed up a little, the Children of Iblis had screwed up a lot. They were zealots, and zealots relied on fear to weaken enemies and blind their followers.

But I wasn't afraid.

My eyes were wide open. I was going to keep Sam and Gemma safe. I was going to destroy the Children of Iblis.

Even when things hit too close to home.

Even when curveballs knocked me flat.

Even when it meant facing down a psychotic cult on the bridge Quinn Johnson had jumped from just a few days ago.

I wasn't afraid.

18

By 12:20 Tuesday afternoon, I was in the middle of the Baker Street Bridge, standing on the pedestrian walkway with a plywood construction barrier between me and six lanes of car-clogged asphalt. Whitecaps danced over Las Almas Bay 824 feet below. The wind off the water was strong enough to knock me backward into the barrier like a warning. And since the Baker had hosted more than its fair share of deaths—intentional and otherwise—it was a warning I'd do well to heed.

My stomach flopped like a one-winged gull as I peeked over the rail. I didn't do heights. Never had.

I whispered a prayer for Quinn into the wind and dialed Emmet.

"Finally got yourself in enough trouble to call, huh?" He sounded playful.

I stepped back from the rail, curled my hand over the mouthpiece to shield it from the wind. "Nah. Still working on it."

The warmth in Emmet's chuckle spread through me like a tonic.

"Listen," I said, "I need to know more about the papers that walked out during the last Archer Construction break-in. Are there any details you forgot to mention the other day?"

Emmet was folding his lip. I knew it like I knew I didn't want to be on that bridge.

"What makes you ask?"

I looked left, saw a cyclist in full racing gear coming toward me.

"I talked with Quinn Johnson's brother," I said. "He mentioned that Quinn started acting different after the insider break-in. Scared."

"What else did he say?" Emmet asked. The cyclist was getting close.

"Not much. He's just a kid. He's upset."

"Not much isn't nothing."

I did some lip folding of my own.

"He wants me to prove his brother didn't kill himself."

Emmet let out a low whistle. "That's a big ask."

"It's why I need your help. Did the cops tell Quinn's family what he said to the woman before he jumped? About Sam being safe?"

"No one knows except the woman and us," Emmet said. "The higher-ups decided it would complicate things if word spread, and since the coroner ruled his death a suicide, that's how they want to keep it."

The cyclist was thirty yards away. I reached into my bag, fastened the blackjack's strap over my good wrist.

"You should tell them, Emmet. They deserve to know."

The cyclist whizzed past. A heavy gust of wind hit, whistling across the phone's mouthpiece, lifting my hair toward the steel cables overhead.

"Where are you?" Emmet said. "A wind tunnel?"

Suddenly, more than anything else in the world, I needed for him to know where I was. At least that way, if I died, they'd know to drag the bay for my body.

"I'm on the Baker," I said.

"What?" he shouted. "Why the hell are you out there?"

"Tell me who the unopened envelope was from. The one stolen from the construction trailer."

A hooded figure with a familiar stride was jogging straight at me on my right.

Blondie.

"Scarlett, what's going on?"

I tightened my grip on the blackjack again. "Tell me who sent the letter, Emmet."

Another jogger was coming on my left. This one was big. Tall big. Thick big.

"Get yourself off of there first," Emmet said. "It's too windy for anyone to be out on that walkway today!"

I hitched the straps of my backpack over both shoulders.

"Emmet?"

"All right, all right," he muttered.

I heard papers shuffling, felt my heart pound in my ears like the waves back onshore.

"That's weird," he said. "The envelope was from Hammett House. The secretary remembered because she couldn't figure why anyone in juvy would bother writing to a big-deal architect."

"Thanks, Emmet. I owe you."

Blondie had gotten too close to keep talking.

"Scarlett, don't you..."

I hung up. Shoved my phone into the outside pocket of my backpack. And hoped like hell I'd live long enough for Emmet to give me the bawling out I deserved.

※

I took off toward Blondie at a run. She froze, feet leaden on the walkway. Tensed. Then she turned tail and ran. I pumped my legs harder, cursed myself for going so light on muay Thai sessions in the past few months. My muscles burned. My lungs fought for air. Still, I was catching up to her.

Halfway back to land, I pulled close enough to take her out. My blackjack landed solid across her hamstrings. She pitched forward into the outside guardrail. Skull met metal. A funny squeak flew out of her as she hit the ground. She lay still.

One down.

The man behind me was closing in fast, looking nasty as shit on a shoe. Six foot and then some, he had the lumpy nose and thick, hard body of a retired boxer.

Him I did not want to fight.

I jumped over Blondie's crumpled limbs and ran at

an all-out sprint. It was no use; the Goon had me beat, and when he tackled me from behind, it felt like I'd been hit by a mile-long train on an open throttle. My knees smashed into asphalt, then my head. I flipped over just before the Goon came down and crushed the air out of my lungs. The *Shubaak* replica from Manny's dug into my back. I jerked my arms out from underneath his chest and rammed my thumbs into his eyes. He roared, tried to shake me off. I pressed harder. A ham-sized fist swung blindly toward my head. I ducked it, pulled in my knee, and forced just enough space under his tree trunk torso to nail him in the crotch. He let out a roar, jerked back, curled up in agony.

I dragged myself up to standing and crouched in a fighting stance, blackjack cocked.

"Walk away," I said. "And we'll call it a draw."

He rolled to all fours.

"I don't care what Iblis wants," he growled. "I'm gonna kill you and that little brat, too." His eyes were muddy brown. Not a speck of gold in sight.

"Gemma..." Her name slipped through my lips before I could catch it.

The Goon sneered. "Don't worry, I'll make sure it hurts real bad for both of you."

He came at me. My right leg swung up and around, high enough for my shin to nail him in the ear. With the same leg, I aimed a heel strike at his nose. I'd hoped to send bits of skull into the back of his head, but ended up with my foot locked in one of his massive hands instead. He pushed forward, driving me into the guardrail so hard there must have been cartoon stars and birdies circling my head.

"You know how to fly, bitch?" The Goon pressed his forearm into my throat, lifting until I was on the tips of my toes. My backpack caught the rail. The Goon pushed harder, cutting off my air completely. No matter how hard I jerked my head side to side, the pressure against my windpipe wouldn't let up. In a few seconds I'd tap out, and the Goon would toss me into the bay.

Only I wasn't ready to die.

With the last of my strength, I hammered my blackjack into his temple. His arm sagged. I sucked in a breath and rammed my fist into the soft tissue under his chin. His head jerked back. I threw an elbow that opened up a razor-thin gash on his cheekbone. Threw another. Blood spurted as his flesh split wide.

From the look on his face, I knew the Goon wasn't used to seeing his own blood in a fight. It surprised him so much I had time to lash out with another kick. His kneecap gave under my heel. He stumbled, dropped his head like a mad bull elephant. My blackjack arched through the air and crunched into the side of his skull. His eyes clouded over. His face drooped. And then he sank into a pile at my feet.

"Not as tough as you look, are you?" I wheezed, wiping blood from the corner of my mouth. Every part of me hurt. I wobbled. Caught myself. Spit a mouthful of blood onto the ground beside him.

"Just remember, pal, you got your ass handed to you by a girl."

Behind us, Blondie was gone. I pulled off my backpack, checked to make sure everything inside it had survived. *Abbi*'s decoy *Shubaak* was in the big compartment, undamaged. Quinn's phone was there, too, along with mine. More importantly, the safe deposit box key I'd stolen from Reem's *hijab* drawer that morning hadn't come out of my jeans pocket where I'd stashed it. Its ridged edge was a comfort against my palm. I put it back, closed the bag up tight, knelt beside the Goon.

He was still breathing. So I stood and walked away, weak as a prom night chastity pledge, but hell-bent on getting Gemma out of her brother's mess alive.

19

Outbound cars lined up bumper to bumper at the Baker's entrance. I stumbled past them, crossing at the first light. Pain stabbed like a dagger behind my eyes. Diesel fumes and blood mingled in my stomach. I swallowed back the acid in my throat and kept going.

"Get in."

I recognized the voice coming through the rolled-down window of an old VW Bug beside me.

"Get. In."

"Mook?" My voice sounded far away. The passenger door swung open. "We need to go, *akht*," he said. "You aren't safe here."

Cars behind us fired warning shots with their horns.

"I'll be damned," I said.

Mook shook his head. "Not on my watch, you won't."

I got in and slammed the door behind me. Mook hit the gas.

"How did you know where I was?" I asked. My body shivered from the shock of it all.

"I am your *mu'aqqibat.*" Mook's eyes flicked back and forth between the road and his mirrors. He looked dangerously close to being nervous.

"Sure. My guardian angel. How could I forget?"

Mook must have noticed my teeth chattering. He turned a knob on the dash, and a cloud of dust and tepid air chuffed out of the car's vents. "Takes a few minutes to warm up," he muttered.

I shivered some more. Took out my phone and dialed Gemma's number. She didn't answer once. Twice. The third time I left a message for her to call me, hoping like hell she could.

"I think they took her, Mook," I said. "Those psychos kidnapped my client."

His eyes were in constant motion. Nervous energy clung to his movements like bad cologne.

"Hand me a cigarette." He pointed his chin toward the crumpled pack on the dashboard.

"Take me to her aunt's," I said. "I need to make sure she's not there."

"No."

I slumped in my seat.

"Please, *akht*. A cigarette."

I shook out one of the cigarettes and punched down the old car's lighter. Put the cigarette in my mouth. Touched the hot orange coil to its end. Inhaled and got a queasy nicotine buzz. "Here." I handed it over.

"Thank you." Mook took a long drag.

"The same people who killed *Abbi* are after me," I said. "Did you know that?"

His eyes lingered in the rearview. "They are not people."

"Do you know about Solomon's ring and the *Shubaak*?"

"Yes."

"Do you believe they're magic?"

He took another drag and blew it out.

"Of course you do," I said, frustrated. "You think you're an angel."

Mook downshifted and stopped at a red light. "One need not believe in something for it to be true," he said.

"The only thing I believe right now is that I need to find Gemma. They're going to hurt her, Mook, just like they hurt *Abbi*."

The light turned green. He put the car in first and popped the clutch.

"The girl's *Qadar* is her own."

"*I'm* part of her fate," I said, getting angry. "And it's starting to look like she's part of mine. I'm supposed to help her, Mook!"

"*You* are an *Abd al-Malik*," he countered. "It is my duty to keep you safe."

I tightened my grip on my backpack strap. I had no idea how he knew all he did, but I was past caring. At the next red light, I was going to bail.

"Don't," he said, looking at me through a haze of cigarette smoke. The light ahead of us went yellow. The car slowed. And then things went bad all over again.

"*Ya Allah!*" Mook shouted. "Duck!"

I dropped to the floor just in time to hear a hollow-edged *tink* overhead. When I looked up, there was a dart lodged against the front of my headrest, still quivering from the impact.

"What the...?" I popped my head up to look out the window. A gray sedan fishtailed in front of us, but Mook's eyes were still on his rearview. He was hunched over the wheel, knuckles white on the gearshift. "Iblis," he barked. "Get down!"

I dropped as low as I could, wedged myself tight against the seat, and curled into a ball. The car swerved, throwing my sore head against the door. My guts heaved. Mook took a corner in second gear so fast I smelled burnt rubber.

"Is he gone?"

Mook didn't answer. He accelerated, turned hard to the right, harder back to the left. Then we did the same thing all over again. And again. Once more, and he motioned for me to get up.

"Take that thing out and wipe down the headrest." He pointed to the dart. "There are rags in the backseat."

My hands shook as I pulled the dart out and swiped a greasy square of old T-shirt across the pinprick hole it left.

"Where'd you learn to drive like that?" I said shakily.
"Mumbai."

He didn't elaborate. I let it slide and held up the dart. "What should I do with this?"

"Wrap it in the rag, and don't touch the tip. It would be most inconsiderate of you to die after all the traffic violations I just committed to keep you alive."

I bound the dart up tight and set it on the floor of the backseat. Mook's cigarette was down to the filter, making him squint against the smoke in his eyes. I pulled the stub out of his mouth and lit a new one from it.

"Poison darts?" I said.

Mook took a long drag.

"Perhaps."

"Like the one that killed *Abbi*."

"Yes."

Warehouses and abandoned piers flashed by as we drove along the river.

"And that was Iblis behind us?"

Mook nodded.

"As in Iblis the jinn?"

He shrugged. "Iblis takes many forms."

Mook was back to being cryptic. It made me feel better.

"You're not going to help me find Gemma, are you?" I asked.

"No."

"Then at least take me to get the *Shubaak*. As an *Abd al-Malik*, I'm entitled to that."

He tucked his cigarette into the corner of his mouth and put both hands on the steering wheel. At the next light, he pushed the turn signal down and headed inland. "Where is it?"

"Las Almas Teachers Credit Union," I said. "Central branch."

"Very well."

"Thanks, Mook," I said after we'd driven awhile. "For everything."

"I do as I must," he answered.

"Don't we all," I said.

"Don't we all."

20

The dog from Calamus was in front of the Laundromat when we pulled up, watching Mrs. Soo waddle past in knee-highs and a lime-green housecoat.

"That dog is following me," I said.

Mook didn't say a word. Hadn't, in fact, since I'd taken the real *Shubaak* out of *Abbi*'s safe deposit box and put it in my backpack. It seemed right, having it with me, though I couldn't say why. Maybe I really was an *Abd al-Malik* and needed the bottle to feel like I was doing my job. Or maybe I just wanted it in case I needed leverage to keep Gemma safe. After all, no antique was worth a little girl's life.

But I had no intention of giving the *Shubaak* up easily.

"Did you hear me, Mook? I said that dog is following me."

He motioned for me to stay put, got out of the car, and came around to my door. When I looked up, I saw the Mook I used to know—the one who'd sit next to *Ummi* on a park bench while I ran around the playground, just because. The one who snuck date-stuffed *maamoul* cookies to me when *Ummi* wasn't looking.

He opened up his coat and motioned toward his chest. I threw myself up and against him with enough momentum to bring down a linebacker. His thin body held, his arms wrapped the duster closed over my head. I smelled leather and cigarette smoke, felt the wiry muscles of his chest under my cheek.

He took off fast and hoisted me over the curb with barely a break in stride. A few steps later I heard the bell on the Laundromat's door, smelled soap and heat and stale coffee. The duster opened. We were facing the back bank of washers, with Mook's body between me and the window. Mrs. Soo's lips mashed together in disapproval. She muttered something in Korean and went back to folding the pair of tighty-whities in her hands.

"I'm going to my office," I said, making for the back stairway. Mook pulled me back by my bad wrist.

"It isn't safe, *akht*."

"But we ditched them. They don't even know we're here!"

He gave me an annoyed look. "Do you honestly believe I haven't noticed the two women following you?"

I was still too worn out from the bridge to pout.

"You mean Shorty and Blondie?" I said. "They're just keeping an eye on me. Or trying to, at least."

Mook frowned. "We're going to my apartment."

Mrs. Soo's mouth pinched so tight that the rest of her face puckered in around it. If I hadn't caught sight of the hooded shape outside, putting a long cylinder to its mouth, she might have made me laugh. Instead, I clotheslined Mook across the chest and dropped both of us to the ground.

"*Ibn il-kalb!*" he cursed as a dart *tunk*ed through the window.

"Sorry." I rolled over and stared up at the thing, sticking out of the wall, dead-on at head level.

"Move!" he barked. "Stay low and get to the supply closet."

I dragged myself across the floor, Mook close on my heels. He reached up when we got to the door, turned the knob, pushed me into a tiny room stacked high with little boxes of detergent and fabric softener. Beyond that was a metal door, triple-locked and heavy enough to keep out a zombie apocalypse.

Mook kicked the first door shut behind us and made quick work of the locks on the second. It swung open into a black, lightless space.

"Go!" He shoved me inside.

"What about Mrs. Soo?"

"They don't care about her. She'll be fine."

I felt blindly for something, anything, to help me get my bearings.

"You're in my apartment," Mook said. "There's a light switch on the wall above you. Bolt the door as soon as I'm gone and don't open it for anyone."

"Wait . . . where are you going?"

"Back," he said. The door thudded closed. I slammed the three locks home, one after the other. Sank to the floor. Let the numbness in my heart spread to skin and muscle and bone. The dark was empty. Quiet. I willed myself to be the same. My eyelids sagged. Right up until the ring I'd set for Gemma's phone split the silence in two.

"Gemma?" I said, too loud.

"Iblis is not pleased with you, girl," came the spear-tipped response.

I sat up straight against the wall behind me. "Who is this?"

"Don't tell me you've forgotten already. We only just left each other on the bridge."

Blondie.

Knowing she was out there, that she had Gemma, gave me the kick start I needed to flip back into detective mode.

"How's the head?" I said, channeling my inner smartass.

She gave an ugly laugh.

"I know you think you're funny, but Hashim will take care of that soon enough."

"Is he tougher than the guy on the bridge?" I asked. "Because that guy's lucky I let him keep breathing."

"That *was* Hashim." Her words curled at the corners like toxic smoke. "And you've made him very, very angry. He's coming for you, girl, even though Iblis ordered him not to. In fact, you'll be lucky if he doesn't tear your little friend apart."

The last bit hit me like a quick left hook. "Where is she? Where's Gemma?"

"Safe. For now. But if you cross us, we'll kill her."

"What do you want?"

"Personally? You. Dead."

"Too bad your boss doesn't have better aim, then, or I would be."

Her throaty giggle made my skin crawl.

"Iblis never misses, fool."

"Well, he did today. Now tell me what *he* wants."

"You are an *Abd al-Malik*. Guardian of the *Shubaak*. What do you think he wants?"

I felt my backpack for the outlines of the decoy and the real *Shubaak* inside.

"I don't know."

"You're a poor liar, and the little girl will die a bad death because of it. Good-bye."

Panic ripped at my gut. "Wait!" I shouted.

"Yes?"

"I can get you the *Shubaak*."

"That's better. When?"

My head spun.

"Friday," I said.

"Friday is fine if all you want for your trouble is a corpse."

"Tomorrow, then. Midnight."

"Better."

"At Woolrich Station," I said, thinking there were always people at the city's main train depot. "Under the clock in the main concourse."

"The Parker," she countered. "Midnight. Oh, and Scarlett?"

"What?"

"Do look out for Hashim."

The line went dead.

I thought about screaming. Hitting the walls. Weeping. Problem was, I didn't have the energy for it. Or the time.

Instead, I dug around for Quinn's phone and pulled up Iblis's photo stream. Gemma was there in a new post, face streaked with tears, eyes terrified. They hadn't added a caption. Hadn't needed to. Iblis's message was perfectly clear.

And I was going to make him regret it.

As I sank into the cushions of Mook's couch, my aching brain warned me not to go to sleep with a concussion. I told it to shut up and leave me alone. Fortunately, it did. And when I came to five hours later, it wasn't holding a grudge.

The apartment was small and windowless, with furniture salvaged from street corners and a thick, permanent cigarette fug. A pizza box sat on the coffee table next to me. *Didn't want to wake you. Bon appétit* was scribbled on the box in Mook's messy hand. Inside, the pie was almost warm. My stomach balked when the yeasty, cardboard smell hit my nose. Then it remembered I hadn't eaten anything since breakfast, and reconsidered.

Turned out not getting killed was hungry work.

Once I'd wolfed down three slices, I went into the bathroom and found jeans, an oversize men's oxford shirt, and polka-dotted boy briefs draped over the edge of the tub. The shirt was Mook's, the rest had come from the load of clothes I'd left in the Laundromat's washer earlier. I brushed my teeth with my finger. Took a bath so hot it nearly made me cry. Then got dressed and called my sister.

"It's about time, Lettie," Reem said over the hospital's background music of voices and beeps.

"Sorry. I was sorting through some stuff over at the office and forgot to look at the clock. I should probably just sleep on the couch here...."

"I know," she said. "Mook phoned to tell me you were there. Is the laundry done?"

I looked down at my jeans and smiled to myself, thinking Mook might not be such a bad guardian angel after all.

"It's done."

"Good. Get some sleep," Reem said. "I start a double shift tomorrow, so I won't see you till Friday."

"I'll sleep if you do," I said.

Reem laughed. "Of course. Oh, and, Lettie?"

"*Hmm?*"

"We're going to *Jumu'ah* prayers together."

"I'd like that," I said. And it was true. Because even though I wanted Gemma home safe and Solomon's ring in my pocket and the Children of Iblis destroyed, what I *needed* more than anything else was to stay alive long enough to pray with my sister on Friday.

"Good," she said. "Love you."

I started to say the words back, but they caught in my throat like oversize pills. By the time they came out, Reem was gone. *Tell her yourself at the mosque*, I thought. Then I checked to make sure the *Shubaak* and its decoy were still in my backpack, put on my boots, stepped into the supply closet, and braced to face down whoever—whatever—was waiting for me outside.

21

The door to the Laundromat opened an inch and stuck. I pushed harder, felt whatever was blocking it give just enough for me to slip a hand through.

"Mook?"

I pushed harder. Visions of my friend, dying in agony like *Abbi* had, poison shutting his organs down, flashed through my head.

"Mook!" I slammed my hip into the door over and over until the resistance gave.

It wasn't Mook on the other side. It was the dog.

By the chilly light of the bare bulb over the laundry sink, I could see her broad head and brindled coat. Her bad ear hung at a crazy angle from its stump of connective tissue and skin, and her single, smart eye was too human by half.

I shrank back. *Ummi* had taught me dogs were dirty and dangerous. They were fine for sniffing bombs and guarding sheep, but keeping them in the house was out of the question. I'd never been allowed to pet them at the park. Not even the little fuzzy ones with bows on their ears.

This dog didn't have bows on her ears.

"Go away." I pressed my back against the doorframe.

She didn't budge.

I took a step out of the closet.

She growled, low at first, then louder. I moved back. The growl stopped.

"I have to leave," I said.

She shifted, toenails clicking against the linoleum floor. There was something sympathetic in the gesture. Sympathetic, but unyielding.

I tried going forward again. She growled again.

"Fine." I retreated into the closet. "Be that way."

She sank to her haunches, calm as a four-legged Buddha.

I waited.

She dropped to her belly.

"Stupid dog," I said.

Her muzzle settled onto her paws.

"You suck."

I wasn't going anywhere.

It stung, calling Deck for help, but with the dog on guard outside and Mook gone, I had no choice.

"You have to stay there," he said as soon as he picked up.

"How did you know what I wanted?" I was angry he'd gotten a jump on me already.

"Mook told Ma what's going on. He said you'd try to get me to help you tonight and..."

"And what? What else did Mook say?"

"He said if I did, they'd kill you."

"He's full of shit."

"He's your *mu'aqqibat*."

Mook had come through for me. Wait. Scratch that. Mook had come through for me huge, saving my ass and helping me get the real *Shubaak* from the bank. But Deck's words still chafed like burlap pants.

"With all the awful stuff that goes on in this world," I said, "all the nasty ways people suffer and die, you're telling me you believe in guardian angels?"

Deck didn't answer right away. I thought about his lips, how close they must be to the phone, how they'd feel against mine.

"You can't die," he said. "You and Manny are the *Abd al-Malik*. You're too important."

"That's crap," I shot back. "Any East Side gun thug can guard an old bottle. Call one of *them*. Because, to tell you the truth, I care a hell of a lot more about my client right now than about some stupid hunk of metal."

Deck was quiet.

"Are you even listening?" I said. "She. Will. DIE. And you know what? I won't be able to live with myself if I let that happen."

"Then you understand exactly how I feel."

The slow smolder behind his words caught me off guard. I hated being caught off guard.

"Just come distract the dog," I said. "Bring a steak or something. Gemma needs me."

"That's her name?"

"Yeah. She's nine, Deck."

He chewed on that awhile before he came out and said what he wouldn't before.

"Mook told us they're watching you. Two women, waiting outside. If I go over there by myself in the middle of the night, they'll try to kill me."

It was my turn to chew.

"Mook knows you can't stay in the apartment much longer," Deck said. "He wants me and Ma to get you out."

"When?"

"Tomorrow. You just have to be patient."

"Sure," I snorted. "That's really my thing."

"For tonight, it has to be," he said. "We've got stuff to get, things to arrange. It all takes time. Just give us until tomorrow afternoon."

"Too long. Not an option."

Deck sighed. "Of course not. Nothing ever is unless you're in charge, right?"

I didn't answer. The silence between us grew dense. Stubborn.

Deck broke first.

"You know that thing I didn't say last night?"

My pulse sped up.

"I meant it."

I broke back.

"I know. So did I."

"I'll get you out as early as I can, okay?"

I took a deep breath. "This isn't just a case, Deck. It's my life."

"Mine too," he said quietly.

"First thing tomorrow. Promise me."

"I promise."

We left the rest unspoken and hung up at the same time, together. Then I lay back down on the couch, and waited to see whether sleep or dawn would find me first.

22

"Her name is Jones."

Mook was on a stool next to the Laundromat's front door. It was 7:14 AM, and the sun was out.

"Go away," I told the dog for the millionth time. She sniffed the narrow crack between the door and its frame and gave me a broken-tailed wag.

"Why won't she leave me alone?" I asked.

"Manny must have sent her to protect you. He has a way with animals." Mook turned the page of his book. Held it high enough to keep anyone on the street from seeing his lips move when he spoke.

Jones let me widen the crack just enough to see

through the Laundromat's front window. A dark-haired woman in jeans and an orange construction vest leaned against a utility truck outside, watching a fat man wheel cases of tomato sauce into DiSanti's. The clothes suited her. Better than the rags she'd worn outside Calamus, at least. And today, she wasn't swaying.

Nuala.

The dog's head swiveled toward the window. I looked down at her shoulders, saw the scars crisscrossing them like a road map. My hand slipped out of the closet, slid cautiously down her back, over knotted sinews, bristly hair, and ribs. I'd never pet a dog before. She didn't seem to mind.

Other than Nuala being there, things on Carroll Street looked the same as they did every morning. Felt the same, too, which was all wrong. There was no sign of Blondie. Shorty, either. I called Decker. He didn't answer. It was 7:19.

At 7:21, a bowlegged woman rounded the corner from Fifty-Fourth. She cut in front of a cab, ignored the driver's tantrum. Tired circles darkened the skin under her eyes, but she carried her laundry basket high on her hip, as if the clothes inside were going to get washed whether they liked it or not.

Mook nodded hello as she walked into the Laundromat. Jones sniffed her ankles. The woman ignored the dog and opened the door of an empty washer. Jones shambled back to her post.

"Hello, Scarlett," the woman said, loading the machine with her back to the windows.

"Hi, Delilah."

She started the machine, settled into a folding chair, and pulled a magazine out of her purse.

"Delilah?"

She tore a page out of the magazine.

"I'm sorry I nearly got myself killed last night, and I promise I won't ever do it again."

"Liar."

She was pissed.

"Are you going to at least tell me how I'm supposed to get out of here?"

Delilah sighed and turned a page. "I suppose."

"Today?" I asked.

She smiled to herself.

"Do you know who owns this building, Scarlett?"

"No, but…"

"Hush up and listen for a change."

I held my tongue.

"Manny owns it," she said.

My tongue got away.

"They put this thing up more than thirty years ago, Delilah."

"*They* didn't. *Manny* did. Designed it himself. He's responsible for every last nook and cranny, right down to the tunnel underneath us."

I kicked back the ratty braided rug under my boots. Saw a solid metal disc embedded in the floor. Solomon's knot was engraved on its surface.

"Son of a bitch!" I said. "This has been here the whole time!"

Delilah's smile turned downright smug.

"Now," she said, "you're going to climb down the ladder below that lid to a vault that's connected to the city's old sewer system. Decker's waiting. He'll wrap you in ventilation tubing, push you up through a manhole to Nuala, and she'll load you into the back of that truck you see out there. Then the three of you will drive away, easy as pie."

I thought of the pie I'd ordered at Rita Mae's, how it had never shown up.

"Delilah?"

"*Hmm?*"

218

"How long have you known about all this? About the ring, I mean, and the Children of Iblis?"

"Feels like forever, hon."

"So you knew they killed *Abbi* for some stupid bottle?"

"Don't you ever say that," she snapped. "Your father died defending us all."

"From what?" I said. "Old mumbo jumbo about magic rings and genies?"

In the harsh glare of the fluorescents, Delilah suddenly looked old.

"Scarlett," she said heavily, "you know what *Abd al-Malik* means, don't you?"

"Servant of the King," I said.

"That's right. Servant of the King. Only the king we're talking about died a long time ago. What your father served—what *we* serve—is an idea. A faith in wisdom and courage and the goodness of human-kind."

I reached out and ran my palm down Jones's back again.

"I miss him, Delilah. *Ummi*, too."

"I know, hon. But they'd be real proud of you if they were here. Real proud."

I was glad she couldn't see me choke up, glad for the feel of Jones's fur beneath my fingers.

"Now," Delilah said, back to her usual cantankerous self, "even though it's against my better judgment, let's get you the hell out of here."

❈

I stood over the open trapdoor in the supply closet and stared down into nothing. *Abbi*'s decoy and the real *Shubaak* were wrapped in an old pair of Mook's socks inside my backpack. The flashlight under my arm was on. I went down the ladder until my feet hit dirt. Shone the beam around. Took in the vault's wet stone walls and cloying smell of old, dead things.

Cockroaches scattered ahead of me. Gravel crunched under my feet, loud as gunshots. I passed into a narrow hallway. Tried not to think about morgue refrigerators or coffins or fresh-dug graves.

The hallway came to a sharp turn. I stopped and gave myself a pep talk. *It's just Decker down here with you. You're fine. You're fine.*

When that didn't help, I grabbed hold of my fear, twisted it until it felt more like anger, and used it to propel myself around the corner. That's when I hit a wall. A living, breathing wall.

I jerked away, smashing my head against the bricks behind me. My flashlight clattered to the ground.

"It's about time you got here."

The flashlight's beam rose as the shape in front of me picked it up. Deck's grin came into view, lit from the chin up like a kid telling ghost stories around a campfire. He was laughing.

"Funny, jinn boy," I grumbled. "Real funny."

He took my hand. Suddenly the tunnel didn't feel so lonely. And Deck wasn't laughing anymore.

He pressed his lips to the top of my head.

"I was so worried about you," he said. "I wish this whole mess would just go away."

I held him close. "Well, it won't."

"I know."

"I have to fix it. You know that, don't you?" The tightness in my throat sliced my words down to slivers.

"Yeah."

I closed my eyes, felt his fingertips travel along the curve of my jaw.

"You're amazing," he said.

"Funny. I was about to say the same thing about you."

He smiled. Leaned in. Kissed me, lips barely parted.

It wasn't a kiss that was meant to lead anywhere; it was a world all its own, complete and whole. For just that one, brief glimpse of forever, I gave myself to someone else.

Decker pulled away first.

"We have to go." His fingertips lingered on my collarbone.

"Yeah." I sighed and took my flashlight from him. "I suppose we do."

Thirty feet later, we were standing beneath an open manhole with a long stretch of flexible ventilation tubing on the floor in front of us.

"Safety orange isn't really my color," I said.

Deck didn't smile.

"You shimmy in, I hoist you up, Nuala pulls you out." He sounded serious. Looked that way, too.

I glanced up at the manhole.

"Have you seen her arms?" I said. "They're like undercooked spaghetti. How's she supposed to lift me out of here?"

Decker laughed with the kind of confidence I needed to hear.

"Don't worry about Nuala. She's tougher than me and twice as stubborn as you. She'll get you out."

"You sure?"

"Trust me," he said. "Trust her."

"Trust is hard when you're used to taking care of yourself," I said.

"I know, but survival's a team sport. Now get in."

I dropped to my hands and knees and wriggled into the tubing, arms wedged tight against my sides. The *Shubaak* and its twin pressed into my back, uncomfortable as truth.

"Stay still." The plastic distorted Decker's voice. "Once you're on the truck, we'll drive to a utility garage, switch cars, and head to Calamus. Don't move until I give you the all clear. Got it?"

"Got it."

"Good. And, Scarlett?"

"Yeah?"

"You're gonna be fine."

Arms scooped around my middle and lifted, as easy as if the pipe were empty. It was disorienting, moving straight up without seeing where I was going. Worse than a fast-moving elevator, better than a cheap carnival ride. Vertigo kicked in, all wrapped up in the smell of vinyl and the ugly feel of losing control.

I'm coming, Gemma. The thought steadied me, kept me from fighting against the walls of my orange prison.

I'm coming.

23

After the initial lift, Deck jerked me over his head, shifted his hands, and pressed into my belly. Air flew out of my lungs so hard I barely heard him tell me to fold. I tucked my chin, jackknifed my nose to my knees. Hands grabbed me by the hips from above. I rag-dolled to make the tube seem empty. Traffic sounds filtered in. My spine scraped the lip of the manhole.

Once my head cleared the hole and Nuala started lugging me sideways, my vertigo eased. I gritted my teeth and waited for my body to hit the bed of the truck.

Nothing happened.

Everything stopped.

Hanging there, helpless and blind, I heard a livid string of curses break free from Nuala and hang like thunderclouds. Then I was moving again, fast, until my shoulder and hip hit metal so hard my teeth smashed together with my tongue between them. Coppery blood filled my mouth, but the feral sound of a dog in full attack distracted me from the taste.

"MOVE!" Decker's voice boomed. Slamming truck doors sent painful vibrations through the bruised pulp of my body. The engine rumbled to life. Something smashed into my side. Shuddered. Lay still.

My thoughts skittered and slid as the truck took off. Too many people were taking too many risks, and it was all my fault. I should have listened to Reem. Gone to college. Been a good girl. But I hadn't, and now people I cared about were getting hurt.

The truck settled into the stop-and-go rhythm of city traffic. We inched along, idling for minutes at a time, making slow progress toward a destination I'd had no say in choosing. Most of an eternity passed before the orange light around me went dim and the truck stopped.

Please be Decker and Nuala, I thought as the truck doors opened. *Please, please, please . . .*

"All clear."

Decker's voice was the sweetest sound I'd ever heard.

I started to wriggle out of the tube. A low growl rose from the shape beside me.

"We're the good guys, old lady. Take it easy," Decker said.

Then came Nuala's voice. "All clear, Scarlett."

I cleared the pipe and slid off the back of the truck, wincing at the raw burn in my shoulder and the grinding pain in my hip. I was banged up and felt like hell, but I was alive.

We were inside a large metal building, empty except for a muddy backhoe and a green pickup with tinted windows. Decker stood nearby, looking away while I tugged my shirt down from around my rib cage.

"Lovely to see you again, Scarlett." Nuala sounded as if we were meeting for tea at Calamus. "My apologies for the roughness back there. Turns out there was a bit of nasty lying in wait for you outside the Laundromat. If it weren't for Jones, you'd not be alive now."

Decker looked into the bed of the utility truck and shook his head.

"What's wrong?" I said.

"She's not going to make it."

I walked over and stared down at Jones. She wasn't panting anymore. She was barely breathing.

"It was all her back there," he said. "The two women Mook told us about were gone, but there was a man. We didn't even know he was there until he came at you. Jones did, though. She took him down and got knifed for her trouble. You'd better thank her while there's still time."

I moved closer to the dog. White rib bones shone through a six-inch gash on her side. One rear leg twisted off at a sickening angle, and her pale tongue hung, limp, out of a muzzle so blood soaked I couldn't see the wound. Still, her eye was half-open, and her tail thumped at the sight of me.

"It's my fault," I said, choking on the words.

"It's nobody's fault," Decker said. "Jones was born a fighter, and from what I've heard, she's won more rounds than she's lost."

I climbed back into the truck bed and knelt beside Jones's crumpled body. Whispered "thank you" into her ear. She struggled to lift her head. I stroked her matted fur. "You didn't have to do this." Her empty socket wept. The warm brown eye next to it searched my own.

I saw life in there—too much to give up on.

"Please don't die," I whispered.

Her tail thumped again, harder.

That sealed the deal.

"We're taking her to the hospital," I said.

Decker shook his head. "We're going to Calamus. Jones is a good soldier, and she's earned a good death. It's time to let her go."

"Bullshit," I said. "Reem can save her."

Deck started to say something. I cut him off.

"Look, I know you want me to find Solomon's ring and the *Shubaak*. I know I'm supposed to be some kind of *Abd al-Malik* warrior princess. But this dog saved my life. I owe her."

Deck shook his head. "You don't..."

"Yes, I do," I said. "So the sooner you get me to the hospital, the sooner I can get back to work. And I gotta tell you, without me, Manny's chances of getting his ring back are looking pretty slim. I know some things you don't, and it's only a matter of time before I find the damned thing."

It was a bluff. Truth was, I only had a lead and a hunch and less than sixteen hours to follow them. But Jones had been willing to give her life for me, and I had every intention of giving it back.

"Help me out here, Nuala." Decker looked to Nuala for support. Nuala was eyeing Jones.

"You can find the ring?" she said.

"I can."

She tapped her lips with her index finger. "What about the *Shubaak*?"

"You'd be surprised what an *Abd al-Malik* like me can pull off," I said, feeling things tip my way.

The gold in her eyes shone.

"And what will you tell your sister about this dog?"

"The truth. That Jones was in a fight."

"You can't be serious!" Decker looked ready to bust a gut.

Nuala eyed him, sober as a Sunday school teacher. "Nobody followed us, Decker. Jones saw to that. As long as we stick to side streets, I think we'll be fine."

Decker kicked an empty plastic oil bottle toward the backhoe.

Nuala turned to me. "Are you sure your sister will treat a dog?"

"Pretty sure," I lied.

"And you know she'll be there?"

"Uh-huh."

"Very well." Nuala had reached a decision, and

Deck's opinion was no longer required. "Let's get the dog to the pickup, then, shall we?"

Together, she and I slid a tarp underneath Jones's body and carried her over as gently as we could. She didn't whimper, didn't whine. I almost wished she would.

Nuala pulled keys out of her pocket and headed for the truck's cab. "Let's go, Decker," she called over her shoulder. "You can ring Manny on the way to let him know where we are."

Deck didn't move. I walked back to him. Put my hand on his arm.

"Survival's a team sport," I said. "Remember?"

He didn't think I was funny at all. Not one little bit. But he let me lead him to the truck, and didn't fight it when I slid in beside him and laced my fingers through his.

※

We dropped Nuala off by the ER to save ourselves the trouble of explaining her to Reem. Then we drove around to the staff lot and found my sister by its gate, med bag and bucket in hand. A thin, scarred man with a junkie's nervous vibe stood next to her. Reem waved to us. The man started to bolt. She stopped him, fished a bill out of her pocket, and gave it to him. Knowing my sister, it was at least a ten.

Decker eyeballed the guy so hard he nearly ran into the gate's lowered security arm. Reem slapped the hood of the truck to stop him. "Easy, big guy," she said, swiping her ID through the gate's card reader. The arm lifted. "Go park in that corner over there." Deck did. Her friend evaporated. Reem followed us.

"What happened?" She was at the back of the truck, staring down at Jones, before Deck and I made it out of the cab. Normally she'd have been all over me like stink on a skunk. But just then, a living creature was suffering, and suffering was Reem's Kryptonite.

"She was in a fight," I said.

"I can see that, Lettie."

Her tone told me I was walking a fine line in clown shoes, as if I didn't already know.

"I didn't see what happened," I said. "This is how I found her."

It was true. Evasive and disingenuous, but true.

"Was it organized? You know I have to call the police if someone put her in a dogfighting ring."

She glanced over at Decker, who was standing off to the side, trying not to get involved.

"No," I said quickly. "Something did this to her on the street. Can you help?"

Reem looked at Jones again.

"I don't know. I'm not a vet. And why aren't you in school?"

That one was for Deck.

"Scarlett called and said she needed me, so I bailed," Deck said, slick as a buffed nail.

Reem started to fuss, but a weak groan from Jones was all it took to send her climbing into the bed of the truck.

"*La howla wa la khoowata illa billah*," she muttered, reaching into her bag. She came out with a razor, shaved the fur on Jones's leg, and started an IV. Deck held the bag of fluid while she examined the wounds on Jones's exposed side. "Spread those out behind her," she told me, pointing to a stack of absorbent pads folded inside the bucket. I did, then helped roll Jones over. Other than a small gash that didn't look too deep, the second side was clear. "*Alhamdulillah*," Reem whispered under her breath, praising Allah.

"Someone's coming," Deck said, tense as fresh-strung barbed wire.

Reem glanced back. Told us it was just security and went back to work.

"Everything okay here, Doc?" the guard called out. He was a ruddy guy with a gut big enough to be twins.

"We're fine, Dimitri. Thanks for checking." Reem barely looked up. Dimitri shrugged, dragged his blood-shot eyes across me and Decker, and walked away. Knowing the hospital and the neighborhood it was in, he'd probably seen stranger stuff before his first coffee break.

Reem worked for the next hour and a half, cleaning wounds, suturing shredded flesh with the neat little stitches she'd practiced endlessly on chicken breasts and banana skins at our kitchen table. When the gashes were closed, she cut open foil packets of fiberglass casting wrap and sent Deck inside to fill the bucket with water. Then she probed Jones's mangled leg. Jones was too far gone to whimper.

When Deck got back, Reem wrapped the leg in thin layers of cotton padding and wet fiberglass. Then she rubbed her eyes, drew in a long breath, and surveyed her work.

It wasn't enough.

"Hand me that Betadine," she said.

I did.

"This is old, isn't it?" She pointed to Jones's raw eye socket.

"Older than today, I guess," I told her.

Reem clicked her tongue. "What the hell," she sighed, and went back to work, closing the thing for good.

"That should do it. Here." She took out four small bottles, a needleless syringe, and a second IV bag. "They're children's antibiotic samples. Give her two teaspoons by mouth with the syringe, twice a day for ten days. You'll have to keep her at your office, Lettie. *Ummi* wouldn't have let a dog in the house, and neither will I."

"Of course," I said.

She pulled out her phone and grimaced. "I have to go. Are you sure you can handle this?"

"You're kidding, right? Do you see this big guy?" I reached up and squeezed Decker's biceps. "He'd throw himself in front of a train for me. Wouldn't you, Deck?"

He didn't hesitate.

"Yes."

"Good. And, Lettie, you stay away from dogfights, even if it's for a case."

"No dogfights," I promised.

"I'll see you Friday." Reem issued the words like a warning before she turned and headed up the ramp to the hospital.

"Reem?" I said.

She turned around.

"Thank you."

"You're welcome. I hope she makes it."

She started walking again.

"I love you, Reem."

She stopped. Tilted her head. Smiled. "I know," she said. And went inside.

24

"That was sweet."

Nuala stepped out from behind the wall next to the security gate. I couldn't tell if she was being sincere.

"Perfect timing." Deck opened the truck's passenger door. "Let's go."

I reached past him and grabbed my backpack from the front seat. "You two go ahead. I'll meet you at Calamus."

"No way." Deck tried to steer me toward the seat. "It was dangerous enough coming here. We've gotta get you safe."

According to my phone, I had thirteen hours and

change to find Solomon's ring. I didn't know if I could do it, didn't even know if Gemma was still alive. All I had to go on was faith, and that had never been my strong suit. Still, there were two things I did know for sure. The first was that anyone I cared about would be better off without me around. The second was that I cared about Deck. A lot.

It was time to fly solo again.

"All right." I made myself sound huffy, mostly for show. "Just let me go to the bathroom first."

"Nope." Deck snatched me back as I started for the entrance. "We're leaving."

"I have to *go*," I said. "It's not negotiable."

"Fine. I'll come with you."

He started toward the door. I stood firm.

"You do understand why it's called the *ladies'* room, don't you, Deck?" I said.

He didn't laugh.

Nuala rolled her eyes and pushed me forward. "For fek's sake! *I'll* take her. You stay with the dog."

Deck wasn't happy with the arrangement. I could see it in the uneasy way he leaned toward me, the way his hands clenched, unclenched, and clenched again. But he let the deal stand, which would have been great if the whole point of me going inside hadn't been to get away from both of them.

"There's a boy," Nuala said, pushing me toward the hospital by the shoulders. "We'll be back before you know we're gone."

As soon as the automatic doors slid shut behind us, her grip clamped down on me, hard enough to hurt. "Couldn't you have come up with anything better than going to the jacks, love? I thought you were cleverer than that."

I gave her a look like I didn't know what she meant and scanned the hall for escape routes. We were in a quiet wing of the hospital, away from patient rooms and the ER. Most of the doors were shut. Ditching Nuala wasn't going to be easy.

"What I don't understand is why you want to be on your own so badly," she went on. "The Children of Iblis aren't to be trifled with. You're much safer with us around."

I asked her if she'd seen a sign for the bathroom yet. She stopped short and spun me toward her.

"Don't play games, girl." The jagged temper she'd shown at Calamus cut through her maternal act like a razor blade through skin. "Neither of us deserves to be

239

treated like a little girl lost. It's insulting enough when men do it. I won't have it from you."

She never raised her voice or loosened her grip. Nuala could be scary as hell, and I respected her for it.

"There's something I have to do. Alone," I said.

"That's better." She let go of my arm. "Now tell me what it is."

"The Children of Iblis kidnapped the girl I'm trying to help. I have to find her."

She waited for me to keep going. I waited for her to realize I was done.

"Do you know what you're doing?" she asked.

"Almost never."

"Answer the question and don't smart off."

I shrugged. "No. Not exactly. But I'm going to improvise the best I can."

She folded her arms and took a step back. "In that case, I'll not stop you."

Since surprises so rarely went my way, I wasn't a fan. But this one was as welcome as French fries at fat camp.

"What are you going to tell Decker?" I asked.

"You'd be surprised what a good liar I can be." There was a hint of sadness in her smile.

I hesitated.

"What, then?" she said. "Did you want a hug? A pat on the head?"

I shook my head and walked, alone, down the hall, until a nagging tug in my gut made me look back.

"Nuala?"

"What?"

"Take care of him for me. Please."

She smiled, slow and knowing, and gave me a wink. "Don't you worry about that, love. I've a knack for taking care of boys. I've done it all my life."

25

The cabbie who picked me up on the opposite side of the hospital drove fast and didn't talk, which suited me fine. I did my best not to think too much about what might be happening to Gemma, and worked on amping myself up enough to walk straight into the mouth of hell on earth.

Hammett House.

Hammett was where they sent the bad kids. The ones who'd screwed up three times too many and burned through the benevolence of even the nicest juvy court judges. In Las Almas, you weren't afraid of the bogeyman; you were afraid of going to Hammett.

And I probably would have ended up there myself if Emmet hadn't pointed out a different path and booted me down it.

I sure as hell never thought I'd walk in under my own steam. But Hammett was the last card I had left to play—more than a hunch, infinitely less than a sure thing. Quinn Johnson had risked breaking into the Archer Construction trailer for nothing but junk mail and an unopened letter. According to Sam, the letter was useless. And Gemma had taught me, toot sweet, that I should listen when little kids talked.

That left one thing, one little, shreddable thing, that Quinn might have taken with him to the grave: an envelope, stamped with a Hammett House return address.

From the outside, Hammett looked like something straight out of a Gothic novel. Its stone walls ringed a full city block and rose so high that only turret peaks showed over the top of them. Once upon a time, when this was a central part of town, Hammett had been the state's best mental hospital. A real showcase for cutting-edge treatments like forced ice water baths and lobotomies. But the city had expanded south, leaving the old building to be swallowed up by factories and warehouses that sprang up on the cheap land around it.

My driver stopped at the end of the long main drive-way. I stared at the lion heads snarling down from both sides of the wrought-iron gate in front of us.

"Symbolism's a bitch, ain't it?" I said.

"Fourteen fifty," was the cabbie's response.

I paid him. Got out. Watched him pull away. Then forced myself to hit the intercom button.

"We're not expecting any deliveries today," a crackly woman's voice said through the speaker.

"That's okay," I answered. "I don't have any."

"What?"

"I said I don't have any deliveries. I'd like to talk to whoever is in charge, please."

"What is this in regards to?"

"My name is Scarlett. I'm trying to help a young girl in a very difficult situation, and I think someone on your staff might have information that could help me."

It took a while for the voice to come back.

"I'm sorry. No visitors today." The intercom went silent and stayed that way.

So much for talk, I thought, taking a slim leather case out of my backpack. I chose a tension wrench and a pick, slipped the wrench into the old-fashioned key-hole, and wiggled it until I'd figured out which way the lock's cylinder turned. Two minutes later the pins were set and the cylinder spun, smooth as a greased merry-go-round.

It was too easy. Any minor-league thief could have done it, and Hammett was built for kids who'd mastered petty larceny before their ABCs. *Don't think*, I told myself. *Just go.* I took a deep breath and walked inside, past the empty stone guardhouse blocking the view from the street.

Whatever I'd expected to see, the vision in front of me wasn't it.

Hammett sat at the top of a thick, sloping lawn dotted with shade trees and white Adirondack chairs. There were no armed guards, no isolation sheds, no attack dogs on patrol. The main building looked more like an Ivy League college than a prison. Blue-striped awnings shaded its windows. Tennis courts and basketball hoops sat off to the right, and beyond that was a big swimming pool with a slide.

A goddamned slide.

As I watched, a mismatched pair of inmates in jeans and sweatshirts came around the corner carrying conspicuously threatening garden tools. The scarier of the two wasn't much older than me, but had me beat by a hundred pounds and probably a half dozen assault charges. He might have been bigger and meaner, but thanks to the nasty scar running from his temple to his chin, at least I was prettier.

"You ain't supposed to be here," he said when they reached me. He sounded like he knew how to hurt people and enjoyed doing it.

"I need to talk to whoever runs this place," I said.

He looked me up and down, waited for me to squirm. I didn't squirm easy.

"It's not visiting day," he said once he'd figured out the score.

I smiled. Repeated my request.

"Sister don't want company," he said.

Our conversation had stalled, so I turned to the brown-haired girl at his side, hoping I'd have better luck with her. She had a belly the size of a soccer ball, a pickax in her hand, and the look of someone used to being underestimated.

"Will you take me to Sister?" I asked.

The big guy started to say something, but the girl shut him down with a look.

"Why?" she asked.

"Is she inside?"

"Sister's wherever she wants to be." The girl's index finger tapped the handle of her pickax. "People don't mess with her," she said. "Or William messes with them."

The Neanderthal with the shovel grunted. Apparently, he was William. Apparently, he agreed.

"I don't want to mess with anyone," I told her. "I just need help."

Her finger kept tapping. Bluesy trumpet music came from one of the building's upstairs windows.

"Sister likes to help people. William doesn't." The girl's eyes narrowed.

"It's not for me," I said. "It's for a little girl who's in trouble. Bad trouble."

She thought about that awhile, motioned for William to move behind me. "Come on, let's go," she said, and took off toward the main building at a fast, pregnant waddle.

I flashed William one of my finest smiles, the kind nobody could resist. "Shall we?" I asked.

William slid his hand down the shovel's handle, aimed its business end at my gut.

"Tough crowd," I said, and got moving before he felt the need to help me along.

We passed through a big, shiny kitchen, complete with a cooling rack full of fresh-baked bread and a tiny woman piling sheets of lasagna noodles into pans that could have doubled as bathtubs.

"*Todo está bien*, Trini," the pregnant girl said when she looked up. Trini shrugged and went back to her pasta.

Beyond the kitchen was a cheery yellow dining room filled with round wooden tables and a sideboard loaded with snacks.

"Come on." The girl looked back impatiently. I was gawking and dawdling like a tourist.

"Is it always like this?" I asked, brushing my fingertips over a basket of green apples.

"Like what?"

"Nice."

"We're criminals, you know, not animals." She sounded insulted.

"Criminals, huh?" I smiled.

"You think that's funny?" William growled.

"No, William," I said. "I don't think that's funny at all. Do you?"

William's forehead wrinkled. I felt bad for the guy. Thinking probably wasn't something he had to do very often.

"Got a name?" I asked the girl.

"Of course," she said. Her tough act was wavering.

"You don't sound so sure."

"Gaby. My name's Gaby."

Gaby didn't look defensive anymore. She looked young and a little scared and not nearly as bad as she wanted people to think she was. I sympathized.

"Good to know you, Gaby. I'm Scarlett."

She shifted onto her heels and put her hands over her belly.

"You know," I said, "I've always been afraid of this place. But it's nice. Really nice. There aren't even bars on the windows."

"Sister had them removed," Gaby said. "'Cause we all know it's better in here."

"Better than what?"

"Where we came from. A lot of our families aren't real...supportive."

"I bet a lot of them are assholes," I said.

That almost made her smile.

I asked her where everyone else was.

"In class," she answered. "I finished early, and since I'm not supposed to be on my own this close to my due date, William was keeping me company."

For whatever reason, that made me think of Reem. I wondered if she'd gotten enough sleep between shifts, if she'd put anything in her stomach besides coffee since I'd seen her last.

"So are you ready to go or what?" Gaby said.

"Sorry. Yeah. This place just has me a little off my game."

"You and me both," Gaby said. "C'mon."

We went up a narrow staircase at the end of the dining room. The trumpet music got louder. It was Miles Davis. Reem's favorite. *Coincidence*, I thought, reminding myself that I didn't believe in omens. Especially not good ones.

At the end of the hall, Gaby knocked on a pair of French doors.

"Sister?"

The song ended. A new one started up.

"Sister, I'm sorry to bug you, but there's a girl here to see you. I don't know how she got on the grounds. William can get rid of her if you want."

William took a step closer and breathed down my neck.

"Hello?" Gaby said.

"You okay in there, Sister?" William bellowed.

The knob dropped. The door swung inward.

"I'm fine, William. Thank you."

It was Sister, only she didn't look like any nun I knew. In my neighborhood, nuns wore shin-length polyester skirts and support hose. They taught school at St. Rocco's, ran the food pantry, and gave free piano lessons on weekends. We liked them, they liked us, and if it hadn't been for their starched white collars and pale blue veils, you'd have thought they were just nice ladies with lousy fashion sense.

This woman was as frumpy as a spread in *Vogue*. From her sharp-cut linen pants and calfskin boots to the broad cuffs of her gauzy blouse, Sister's whole getup screamed money. Her blond hair was styled in a short, mannish cut, and her skin had the well-tended glow of a woman unwilling to let time decide how far past forty she was going to look. Two chains hung from her neck; one was a cross, the other ended below her collar. Sister was the damnedest nun I'd ever seen.

She tilted her head and studied me calmly. "This is a private facility. You shouldn't be here."

It was the voice from the intercom.

"I'm sorry," I said, "but like I told you earlier, I'm trying to help a little girl who's in a lot of trouble. Do you know about the boy who jumped off the Baker Street Bridge?"

Pain stretched her fine features taut.

"Everyone does. It was a terrible tragedy," she said, too carefully.

"Did you know he didn't want to die? That he jumped to protect his little brother?"

Sister went rigid. Gaby rushed toward her. Hell, I moved closer, too, until William yanked me back. The nun was about to pass out.

"You want me to see her out, Sister?"

"No, thank you, William." Sister's body steadied. The glassy sheen cleared from her eyes. Gaby whispered something in her ear, and Sister patted her arm.

"Let the young lady go, William," Sister said. He did.

Gaby whispered something else I couldn't hear.

"No, dear, I'm fine," Sister said. "You and William may join the others now."

William wasn't happy about that, but he backed off. Sister touched Gaby's cheek.

"You're flushed, Gabrielle."

"I'm fine," Gaby said.

Sister shook her head. "Go lie down. The doctor said you're to rest."

"I have to help William with his math homework."

"All right." Sister sounded too tired to argue. "So long as you stay off your feet and take a nap this afternoon."

Gaby told Sister she would and gave me a look that was more promise than threat. *Don't you hurt her*, it said. *Or I will hurt you more.*

I offered her my hand. She shook it. We weren't so different, Gaby and me.

Once the Hammett House welcome wagon was gone, Sister spoke with the kind of enthusiasm people usually saved for cold soup and wet socks.

"I don't know if I can help you, young lady."

I took out Quinn's phone. Showed her the picture of Gemma that Iblis had posted.

"They're going to kill her, Sister."

"Well then," she said, eyes locked on the screen, "I suppose you'd best come inside."

26

Sister's office was a bright room filled with enough security monitors to put a Vegas casino to shame. There were screens for the front gate, the lawn, kitchen, and dining room, along with classrooms, supply closets, and dormitory hallways. Sister had been watching me ever since I got out of the cab.

She steered me toward a wingback chair and took a love seat for herself. A squat cast-iron teapot, the kind they sold in Japan Town, sat on the coffee table next to a teacup with steam still coming off it. She didn't offer me any. I didn't ask.

"Tell me what you want," she said, blunt as a billy club.

So I did.

"Quinn Johnson stole a stack of mail from a trailer at The Parker's site that belonged to Archer Construction. My theory is that he did it because he was desperate—because a cult called the Children of Iblis was threatening to hurt his little brother if he didn't help them find George Fagin, the man behind The Parker. And whether you want to call it bad luck or good, what Quinn found in that mail was an envelope with a Hammett House return address and a handwritten note from Fagin inside. I think Quinn believed he'd found the person the Children of Iblis were looking for, and that he killed himself to keep his brother safe and George Fagin's whereabouts hidden."

Sister was gray as ashes by the time I finished.

"You're rather direct, aren't you?" she said.

"Yes."

She looked out the window a long, long time.

"Look, Sister," I said. "I don't know why the Children of Iblis want Fagin so bad, but it has something to do with an old legend, an antique ring, and the fact that they honest-to-God believe they're genies. The little girl they took is Arthur Archer's daughter. They've brainwashed his son. Please, please help me stop them."

Sister stood and walked to her desk slowly, as if she'd aged a hundred years. She picked up a framed black-and-white snapshot. Brought it back. Handed it to me without a word.

A pretty blond stood underneath a banner that read: LAS ALMAS MAYFEST PARADE, 1979. The girl's hair hung past her tube top to the waistband of sequined hot pants. She looked exactly like the woman in front of me, only younger. A large gold ring dangled from a chain around her neck.

"This is you?" I said.

Her head dropped. She looked exhausted. Sick of secrets. I knew exactly how she felt. *Abbi* had kept the *Shubaak* secret, *Ummi* did the same with her cancer, and both had died for their trouble. Secrets killed Quinn Johnson, too, and they were making a hard run at Gemma.

Sister's eyes met mine. *Ask me*, they seemed to say. *Ask me and I'll tell you.*

"Where's the ring now?" I said quietly.

She stared out the window some more.

I forced myself to strip off every bit of armor I'd built around myself since *Abbi*'s death and leaned toward her.

"They killed my dad, Sister. And yesterday, they tried to kill me."

"How can I be sure you don't just want the ring for yourself?" she asked bleakly.

"You can't. You'll have to take a leap of faith. It's the only way to save the little girl."

Sister's eyes filled with tears. Her hand moved to her throat.

"My name," she said, tugging at the long chain around her neck, "is Lillian George Fagin. And it's not me they're after. It's this."

⚛

A hammered gold ring hung from the chain, gleaming dully in the afternoon sun. It was simple. Unadorned, except for the raised knot on its face. Sister caught it in her hand.

"So you're him?" I said.

She laughed. Stopped short, like the sound surprised her.

"No. I'm me. But people in the business world don't expect women to make themselves rich, especially not as rich as I am. That's why I use my middle name—George—in my business negotiations. It's easier that way."

I hadn't looked away from her hand yet. Without realizing it, my own had drifted down to my backpack and was resting over the bottles inside. Everything the Children of Iblis wanted, everything they were willing to cheat, steal, lie, and kill for, was in that room.

"I was a pickpocket," Sister said. "A good one. I never got caught, not even when I stole the ring off that man's finger outside Marlowe's department store. It was my seventeenth birthday."

She took a tissue from her pocket. I fought off the urge to snatch the ring from her hand.

"I knew there was something special about the ring the moment I first held it," she went on. "It made me feel stronger. Better. So long as it was with me, every tourist I robbed was loaded with cash, every pocket was full. Some days I didn't even have to work; I'd just find money lying around on the street. Of course, I had always known that stealing was immoral, but doing it to survive never made me feel guilty. Once I'd moved past survival, though, I . . . well, it felt wrong."

"So you went legit?" I said.

"Yes. I bought a magazine stand in the financial district and hired street kids like me to run it. When that little enterprise did well, I bought more stands, then storefronts. Eventually, I started my own venture capital company. The riskier my investments got, the more money I made. I grew very rich very fast."

She started to drift off into memory. I brought her back.

"So rich that you started giving it away?"

"Money used to mean a great deal to me, Scarlett. But now I understand that its real value lies in its power to help others."

"Is that why you took this place over?"

"No. Hammett House is personal. I . . . spent time here as a child. It was awful. So, two years ago, I told the city I was a nun, used my first name in our negotiations, and paid a ridiculous sum for the property. Technically, one of my shadow companies runs Hammett. In reality, it's me."

My phone vibrated in my bag. I eyed Solomon's ring and let the call go to voice mail.

"Tell me about the letter, Sister."

"I wrote it," she said, "to thank Mr. Okoye, The Parker's architect, for blueprints he'd drawn up for a new wing here at Hammett. It was meant to go out on Fagin Inc. letterhead, but Gaby was working with me that day and must have put it in a Hammett envelope by mistake. It was my fault, really. She was just trying to help."

Sister played with the chain around her neck.

"I'm never that careless," she said. "I even paid a clerk to purge all of The Parker's records down at City Hall...."

Delores, I thought. *You cherry menthol–breathed old sneak.*

My phone vibrated again. This time I excused myself and checked it. Saw a close-up on the screen of Reem, hunched over in the back of the truck, working on Jones. TICK TOCK, the message said.

My heart dropped like a broken elevator.

"They found my sister. They found Reem," I croaked.

Miles Davis had stopped playing. Sister watched me, her mouth open helplessly.

Then I saw the message that had come in earlier. From Delilah.

Children of Iblis hit my boy with a dart.

Reem trying to save him.

Nuala kidnapped. Get to Calamus now.

"Scarlett?" Sister whispered.

"They..."

My tongue seized. My eyes stung.

"They might have killed someone I care about very much."

Sister's hand, the one holding Solomon's ring, shook. Tears flowed silently down her cheeks.

"Go, then," she said. "But let me tell you something first."

I listened because, for the moment, there was nothing else I could do.

"Quinlan Johnson came here the day before he died," Sister said. "He told me about the Children of Iblis, how they'd seen sketches of my building, of its skybridge shaped like Solomon's knot, in the paper. Those pictures led them to believe that Fagin—that I—might know the whereabouts of the ring. The poor boy kept going on about armies of genies taking over the world. He asked for my help. He was so scared, but I..."

Her fingers tightened into a fist around the ring.

"When I lied and told him I didn't know what he was talking about, a spark went out inside him. I watched it happen. And I did nothing."

Her fingers opened.

"This isn't mine anymore," she said, looking at the ring. "It never really was."

She pressed the gold into my open palm. It was warm from her hand. Alive. She smiled, as if she'd made a decision, and that decision had brought her peace.

"Take it," she whispered. "Take it and save your friends."

27

illian George Fagin didn't ask if I had a driver's license. She just handed me the keys to a late-model minivan, smiled wryly, and told me not to scratch the paint. Any other time I would have put in a bid for the blue Jag convertible parked nearby in the Hammett garage, but with my whole world falling apart, sports cars just didn't matter.

As I backed the van out, Gaby and William came into the garage. A word or two from Sister was all it took to clear the worried look from Gaby's face. William didn't look appeased. He just looked like William. And he didn't wave good-bye.

Outside Hammett's gates, the first thing I did was call Reem. I needed to hear her voice, to tell her what was going on, and to ask whether Decker was alive or dead. But she didn't answer. She never did while she worked.

And Delilah didn't answer, either. I left a message saying I was okay, and could she please call me.

Emmet picked up right away.

"Scarlett?"

Getting right to the point had worked so well with Sister that I decided to give it another go.

"Reem's in danger, Emmet. You have to protect her."

"Come again?" he said.

I took a deep breath. Stopped at a red light. Looked both ways before I swung a right.

"You remember that case I was working?"

"The Archer Construction kid?"

"That's the one."

"Of course I do. What about it?"

"It went bad. Or good, depending on how you look at things. I'm about to bring down something big, Emmet, and the people behind it would just as soon kill a person as tell them hello. They sent me a picture of Reem at the hospital as a threat. If I don't work this right, they're going to hurt her."

There was no play in Emmet's voice.

"Come in, Scarlett. Right now."

"It's too late for that."

"Scarlett..."

"I mean it, Emmet. They already poisoned my friend Decker, probably with the same stuff that killed my father. He's at the hospital. Reem's working on him."

"What the hell have you gotten mixed up in?" he said.

"Nothing I wasn't meant to. Anyway, it's a done deal now, and I have to see it through to the end. I can't do that if I come in, and nobody else can do it for me."

"This is too much for you to handle alone, Scarlett. I'll put some officers on Reem and come help you. Name the place, and I'll be there."

"Uh-uh," I said. "If they see you, they'll kill Gemma Archer."

Emmet went quiet. He was thinking, and even though I was short on time and temper, I gave him the space to do it.

"I don't want Reem to have to live without you," he finally said.

"I don't, either, but she could do it. She's strong that way, Emmet. It's how she's built. Besides, I'm not going to let them kill me."

"Please don't."

"So you'll help me? You'll keep her safe?"

"No one's going to hurt Reem," he said. "You can be damn sure of that."

"Thank you, Emmet." I hung up before he could get in another word.

Next, I dialed Mook.

"As-salaamu alaikum."

"Wa alaikum as-salaam. Where are you, Mook?"

I could hear his scowl, louder than words.

"Mook, I need your help. The Children of Iblis know where Reem is. My friend Emmet's going to keep an eye on her, but he doesn't understand how crazy they are. Will you watch over her, too?"

"No."

I accelerated through a yellow light.

"Come on, Mook, I don't have time for this. You're a *mu'aqqibat.* Do your job."

The ring thumped against my chest as I hit a pothole.

"I believe you, okay?" I nearly shouted. "I believe you're an angel, and that your job is to protect me. Only right now Reem needs you more. So help her. Please!"

"No."

There was finality in his voice. The kind you don't take back.

"Why?" I demanded.

He sighed. "Because, *akht*, the dance between *mu'aqqibat* and *Qadar* is a delicate one. Mankind has free will, but Allah knows everything that has and ever will come to pass. Only He can say whether it is time for me to lead or to follow."

"This isn't about fate, Mook! It can't be. Reem didn't have any say in what's happening. That means she's not really making choices right now. She has to be able to make choices, Mook, or it's not fair. You have to protect her!"

"Fair has nothing to do with it, *akht*. Reem's *Qadar* is set, and only Allah can know it. Haven't you learned that by now?"

"So you're not going to help." It wasn't a question. I was saying what I already knew.

"I'll help when I am meant to," Mook said. "*Mu'aqqibat* are not put on earth to protect all humans, all the time. We merely prevent them from dying before they're meant to. Whether or not you wake tomorrow morning has already been determined. For now, you are alive, and life is a gift. Use it wisely."

He was gone before I could tell him where he could stick his *Qadar*.

It was probably a good thing.

I swore out loud, looked at my backpack on the passenger seat, and took a quick inventory. I had two bottles, both of which were priceless relics, one of which the Children of Iblis thought was a portal to another dimension. Hell, for all I knew, they might even be right; the real *Shubaak* might open straight into Oz or Narnia or goddamned Middle Earth, for all I knew. I also had two phones, a lock-picking kit, a blackjack, an armed cop on his way to protect Reem, and the best doctor in Las Almas busting her ass to keep Decker alive. What I still *needed* was to make sure Hashim didn't kill me before I got to The Parker. I *needed* to figure out how to keep Gemma alive. I *needed* to tell Decker that I loved him.

And there were only six hours left until midnight.

No problem.

I had it covered.

Slick Eddie's was a pawnshop on the south stretch of Daly where nice people didn't go. It was small and cramped and filthy and smelled like old fish, but the owner had a reputation for not asking questions or checking IDs. He also had a thing for me.

"Evening, Eddie," I hollered. The shop seemed deserted when I walked in, but he was there. Eddie was always there.

"Is that the lovely Miss Scarlett?"

His voice came from behind a crowd of naked mannequins wearing Mardi Gras beads and stilettos.

"It's me," I answered.

Eddie appeared, wearing his usual frayed blue suit. The one covered with stains from God-knew-what that had been there since God-knew-when. His greedy, myopic eyes leered at me from behind glasses thick as bricks.

"It's been a long time since I had the pleasure," he said. "I've missed every luscious bit of you."

"Quit it, Eddie. You're making me blush." I stepped behind a stack of old ammunition boxes, grateful for the foot of space they maintained between the two of us.

"Yes, yes. Well, what can I do for you tonight?" A pale tongue slithered out to wet his liver-colored lips.

I flashed him the stack of bills I'd withdrawn from a

nearby ATM. It was everything Reem and I kept in our checking account. I hoped it would be enough.

Eddie's eyes sharpened behind their lenses. If there was one thing that turned him on more than underage girls, it was working a deal.

"What are you looking for?" he said.

I rattled off my shopping list and took it as a good sign that he let me keep talking.

I shouldn't have.

"I won't sell you a gun," he said flatly. "I could go to jail for that."

"You'd go a lot faster and a lot longer if the cops bothered tracking down where most of your merchandise comes from. This stuff is hotter than lava, Eddie."

"I run a clean shop." He didn't bother trying to sound indignant.

"Up front, maybe," I said. "But what about in the back?"

He licked his lips again. I fought my gag reflex. Nearly lost.

"A wise man once wrote that guns are just a fast curtain to a bad second act," he said. "You looking for a bad second act, Scarlett?"

"I'm looking for any kind of second act at all, Eddie."

Something ugly came into his eyes as they slid over my body, leaving the kind of slime trail you can't wash off.

"Maybe…" he said, dragging the word out, "we could work something out in a trade?"

I pressed my hand against the *Shubaak* in my bag. Facing whatever waited for me at The Parker with a gun would have been nice, but not nice enough for the kind of deal Eddie was suggesting.

"Cash, Eddie," I said. "That's all I'm offering."

"You're sure?"

"I'm sure."

"Pity." He snaked a hand into the deep pocket of his pants. "Then no gun."

I kept my eyes on his, refusing to look down. "Fine. Then let's talk about what my cash will get me."

A reptilian smile spread across his face. His hand came out of the pocket, jangling a loop of keys.

"Right this way, m'dear," he said with one more flick of his tongue. "Follow me."

28

The doors to Calamus were locked when I got there. It was 7:14 PM. I had less than five hours. There were no corner boys slinging drugs on the stoop nearby. No Nuala. No Jones. "Manny!" I pounded on the heavy wooden doors with my blackjack. The sound smacked at my eardrums and ricocheted down the street.

"Manny!"

It was a fool's errand, standing there, yelling, but there weren't many other ways to reach someone who wouldn't answer his phone and never left the house. I looked up and down the street, making sure my racket wasn't drawing any locals. Faces appeared behind windows in buildings that should have been empty, but other than that, I was alone.

"You're in there! I know you are!"

I was just about to give the wood another whack when the sound of a sliding bolt stopped me short. "Hurry up!" I shouted.

The door swung open on its creaking hinges. I expected to see Manny. I ended up with someone different altogether.

"*As-salaamu alaikum.*" Asim's words were hollow as straw. The man who'd stormed into my apartment, bashed up my wrist, and stolen the decoy *Shubaak* was gone. In his place was a shell. Even the gold rings in his eyes looked as if they'd been eroded by worry and tears.

Only grief could carve a man out like that.

"*Wa alaikum as-salaam.* Is he alive?" I whispered.

Asim's face was stony.

"He is."

"*Alhamdulillah,*" I said, weak with relief.

Asim smiled wearily. "Praise to God, indeed. And to your sister, who delivered Allah's mercy. It seems she has made quite a study of poisons and their treatment. I am in your family's debt."

He stepped back and motioned for me to come inside. It wasn't quite an apology for the other night, but I never had cared about the little things.

I told him I needed to see Manny.

"Of course you do." Asim turned and led me through the sanctuary, past Mary's mournful gaze and Eve's knowing smile. This time, no warmth or welcoming scents met us as we descended the stairs behind the chancel. Calamus smelled like cold stone.

Manny was waiting.

"I'm glad to see you, child." There was weariness in his words.

"I'm glad I'm still alive to be seen," I countered. There was no gentleness left in me, but I cracked a smile to smooth my rougher edges.

"You are aware of everything that has transpired?" Manny asked. Asim sank, heavy as a bucket of sand, into one of the dining room chairs. It looked like it took everything he had not to lay his head down.

"I'm not sure," I said. "I know that Decker's in the hospital. Nuala's missing. My sister's safe for now. Other than that, I'm a little in the dark."

"Decker and Nuala were attacked in the hospital garage," Manny said. "We know that a security guard heard some sort of commotion and ran to the scene. Decker was only conscious long enough to say Nuala's name. The guard acted quickly, and with the emergency room so close, Reem got to him in time to shut down the poison's progress. It seems she was able to identify it immediately."

"*Abbi*," I said. "She knew it because of *Abbi*."

Manny nodded. "Yes, child. That's right. And now they're keeping Decker in a coma to give his body the best possible chance to recover. As for my wife..." He closed his eyes. Breathed out heavily. "No one knows what's become of her."

"What about the dog?" I was focused on details. Details were my bread and butter. They were all I had.

"The guard said something about seeing a man, an indigent, apparently, climbing from the back of a pickup truck with a dog in his arms."

Reem's addict.

I wondered what he'd seen, why he'd carted Jones away. With any luck my sister's kindness was being paid forward. Jones, at least, stood a chance.

"Good," I said. "Now, I need your help with some other stuff."

"Then you shall have it, *Abd al-Malik*," Asim said.

I started to say I'd been called worse, but Manny spoke first.

"Do you have the true *Shubaak*, Scarlett?"

I shrugged. "Maybe. But what if I still don't believe all this hocus-pocus?"

"If that is the case, then tell me, what *do* you believe, my dear?"

"Hell if I know," I said.

Manny patted my hand. "Good. I wouldn't trust the *Shubaak* to anyone unwise enough to assume they had all the answers. Especially not at such a tender age."

"*Abbi* had answers."

"Your *abbi* had faith, and even that he did not come to without a struggle of his own."

I chewed on the inside of my lip.

"*Abbi* never struggled with anything."

"I don't lie, my dear," Manny said. "Obfuscate, yes. Lie, never."

"There's a pretty thin line between the two, don't you think?"

"Thinner than you know."

Asim stood up fast enough to send his chair skidding backward against the tiles. It hit the edge of a rug and tipped, crashing into a coffee table.

"Enough!" he said. "I can't listen to this anymore!"

Asim was angry, shaking with all the same emotions I'd clamped a lid on, deep down inside myself.

"My son cares for you, Scarlett. Delilah does, too. And, difficult as it is for me to say, I accept that you are the *Shubaak*'s rightful *Abd al-Malik*. No woman has served since the *Shubaak* passed to Solomon's daughter, never mind a girl. But Manny believes it is your *Qadar*, and so does my son. Out of respect for them, I will believe as well. Tell us if you have the *Shubaak*, *Abd al-Malik*. Tell us what you require. And I will do my best to assist you."

It had taken a lot for him to say all that, and I knew it So I looked at the ground, humble as a monk, and leaned forward on the table before lifting my eyes to his.

"Yeah," I said. "I've got the *Shubaak*. Now tell me how the damned thing works."

29

Las Almas was the kind of town that never shut down all the way. Club music thumped on Rainey Street from supper to sunrise, greasy spoons and Chinese delivery places ran 24-7, drugstores and bodegas kept their doors open all night. But in the financial district, where the outline of The Parker building loomed over lesser buildings below, quiet hugged the streets like a blanket.

I parked Sister's minivan in a loading zone and checked to make sure everything was where it should be. Solomon's ring was still on Lillian Fagin's chain around my neck. The *Shubaak* and its decoy were in my backpack, along with a needle and thread from Manny's medicine cabinet, and my treasures from Slick Eddie's. As for Manny and Asim, they were tucked into their beds back at Calamus, convinced that we were going to take down the Children of Iblis after a good night's sleep and a nice breakfast. It was a lie I'd be glad to atone for later, since dead girls can't apologize.

The fence around The Parker's site was twenty feet high, with a triple strand of razor wire looped over the top for good measure. I walked to the northeast corner of the lot and hunted until I'd found just the right spot to cut with my pawnshop lineman's pliers. I snipped a neat line along a post, climbed through, clamped the flap back in place. By the time that was done, it was 10:30. I silenced my phone and Quinn's, tightened my backpack straps, and looked up.

A hundred yards away, enormous steel skeletons rose out of the dark Las Almas dirt and stretched toward the stars. There were no walls yet, no windows, only an outline of the towers to come. It was a breathtaking thing to see by moonlight. It was a breathtaking thing to see at all.

I scanned for security guards. Nothing moved.

Thirty yards to my right, the shifting glow of a TV danced across a construction trailer's windows. "Stay put," I whispered to the guard inside, and crept past the trailer, past orange plastic netting strung around The Parker's bare flanks, and came to what must have been the building's front entrance. Then I stopped dead.

Four shapes materialized out of the dark. Two were Rottweilers, black as the sky and ten times scarier. The other two were all muscle and teeth, with flattened ears and tails docked down to nothing. Pit bulls.

Adrenaline jacked through me, but I held my ground. These were guard dogs, trained to hurt people who ran when they shouldn't. My best bet was to stay still, give them no reason to charge, and hope I could protect my throat if they attacked.

Seconds passed. Minutes. Nothing happened. The longer I stood there, the less threatened I felt. One Rottweiler sat on its haunches. A pit did the same. The other two sniffed the air, mellow as old men playing chess in the park.

Slowly, slowly, I reached toward my chest for Solomon's ring. The dogs' eyes followed my hand. I pulled up on the chain, feeling like an idiot for wanting fairy tales to be true. The dogs watched. I lifted the ring as high as the chain would go. Their eyes rolled north. I moved my arm sideways. Four heads followed.

No. Freakin'. Way.

My mouth was dry as chalk.

The ring's supposed to give you control over humans and jinn, animals and the weather.

"Sit?" The word came out shaky. Four heads tilted, trying to understand. I tried again.

They sat.

"Lie down?"

Their eyes never left the ring as their bodies settled to the ground.

I took a step forward, told the dogs to stay. They did. I took another. And another. The dogs watched, curious but relaxed. "Stay," I said again. One of the pits scratched its ear.

From there I crept along, cautious as a cat in mittens, navigating the rutted construction mud underfoot. The dogs never moved, not even when I made it inside the building's unfinished atrium.

It was an eerie place. Beams stretched forever overhead. The air was too still. There should have been creaks. Drips. Wind. Anything to break up the silence.

Even my footsteps were noiseless as I crossed the atrium, turned down the outline of a hallway, and stopped in front of a construction elevator. I got inside, closed its gate behind me, and hit the down button. An electronic whine bit the silence. Gears turned.

Six basement levels later, the elevator clanged to a stop, and I got out. Industrial-strength epoxy and paint fumes burned my eyes. My flashlight's beam swept the cluttered darkness, found a line of bare, metal-backed bulbs strung along the walls. I followed their cord to a switch, flicked it on, and squinted against the glare. I'd been expecting a massive, open skating rink. What I found was closer to a half-built maze of concrete support columns and construction materials. Plenty of hiding places, plenty of cover.

It was perfect.

For the next fifteen minutes, I memorized the basement's layout and hid the tools from my backpack on a ledge made by unevenly stacked drywall panels. With any luck, I wouldn't need anything but my brains and my charm.

With any luck, I'd trade a ring for Gemma and walk out of there with the two of us alive.

With any luck, I wouldn't have to rely on luck at all.

The dogs were waiting in a row outside. "Scram," I whispered. They stood up, trotted back a hundred feet, and sat down. I told them they were good dogs.

TV light still flickered in the trailer's window. It was darker now, and clouds had come in thick enough to block the moon and drag the sky low. I kept my flashlight off and stumbled around Porta-Potties and heavy equipment until I found an enormous crane. Its unlocked cab smelled like beef jerky and sweat, but sat high enough to give me a good view of the grounds without anyone getting a good look back.

Inside, with the door shut tight, I stripped off my jeans and took out the sewing supplies from Manny's. Goose bumps dotted my legs. My frozen fingers struggled to thread the needle in the dark. I thought about the flashlight again, decided the security guard's shack was too close to risk turning it on. Thankfully, just as I was about to give up, an icy sliver of moonlight punched through the clouds and shone straight into the cab.

"I owe you one," I said with a glance skyward. Then I worked quick, racing the clouds, to stitch Solomon's ring onto the back fabric of my waistband.

I won.

Barely.

Shivering, I pulled the jeans back on, tugged at the ring to make sure it would hold, and slipped the worn signet ring from Slick Eddie's jewelry case onto my left thumb. It was heavy and gold, and didn't look nearly enough like Solomon's to make me comfortable. But it would have to do.

After that, I waited.

Twenty minutes later, my ass was numb and my hips were as knotted as a box of old necklaces.

Ten minutes after that, the dogs gathered under the crane, staring up like they wanted me to come out and play. "Not now," I whispered. And off they padded to the building's front entrance.

11:50.

Five minutes more.

I spun the signet ring on my thumb. Even with the heat of my skin underneath, it was too cold. Gave me the willies. I took it off and stuck it in my pocket.

At 11:55, I put my backpack on, surveyed the dark yard, and swung down out of the cab. Any decent sniper with a nightscope could have picked me off no matter how fast I sprinted to The Parker, but there was no sense dawdling and making anyone's job easier. I ran, heart in my mouth, *Abbi*'s bottle bouncing against my spine. The dogs didn't come out of the building. No snipers fired. I made it to the atrium and crouched low at the door.

The silence inside was awful.

Here goes nothing, I thought, standing up with my flashlight raised like a club.

Halfway across the cold concrete floor, the sound of a single drip shredded the silence.

I stopped. Turned to look down the outline of the hallway to my left. Something was there, stacked and still as a pile of sandbags.

My eyes strained against the dark.

My stomach lurched.

It was the dogs. Throats slit, tongues lolling from the sides of their mouths, piled on top of each other like so much garbage. Blood, black as oil, pooled on the concrete around them.

I doubled over and threw up, wave after wave of nausea emptying my belly, until even my bile was spent. Then I straightened up. Looked back. Saw a tall, dark shape coming at me fast.

"Scarlett?"

A high beam seared my eyes. I didn't need them. I knew the voice.

"What are you doing here, Emmet?"

He lowered the flashlight enough for me to see his outline again. "Reem's fine. She's got two cops with her."

"That's not what I asked." Doubt clawed at my empty insides.

Emmet took a step toward me.

"Stay back," I said.

He stopped. Furrowed his brows.

"What's wrong with you, Scarlett?"

"How did you know where to find me?" My voice trembled. "Are you one of them?"

"What kind of question is that?" he demanded. "Reem asked me to track you down. You think she doesn't know something's wrong? Your friend nearly died in that hospital parking lot. She's out of her mind, worrying about you. I'm just glad you kept nagging me about The Parker, or I'd never have known where to come."

My thoughts scrambled for footing.

"Are you with the Children of Iblis, Emmet?"

"With the *who*?" he said, coming at me for real.

"Get away!" I backed toward the elevator.

"Scarlett..." He stepped past the edge of the girder blocking the dogs from his sight. His head turned. "What the...?"

The elevator gate clanged behind me. Something hit the back of my head so hard it didn't even hurt. The world started to melt. Emmet was running toward me.

Maybe dying's not so bad after all, I thought.

And then I didn't think any more.

30

Being knocked out was bad. Coming to was worse. White-hot daggers of pain exploded up from the base of my skull. My body was heavy as lead. Just thinking about opening my eyes took more out of me than I had.

"Scarlett?" a woman whispered from a million miles away. "Scarlett! Wake up!"

Somewhere inside my haze, part of me recognized the voice.

"Nuala?" I managed to say.

"Stay quiet, or they'll hear you!"

I peeled my eyelids up, clamped them back tight

against the glare of the construction bulbs around us. My shoulder ached against the cold concrete floor. Behind me, my bad wrist throbbed in time with my heart. I tried to pull it forward. Tried to pull my good one forward, too, but it was no use; I was trussed up tighter than a Thanksgiving turkey.

"Open your eyes," Nuala whispered. "Quick now, before they come back."

I squinted just wide enough to see that she was sitting on the floor next to me, still lovely, even with wild hair and grime-streaked cheeks. There was a support column at her back. Her hands were bound in her lap.

"There's a girl," she said. "Wake up, now."

My pupils struggled to adjust. I remembered the dogs. Fought back a fresh round of nausea.

"Listen, Scarlett, we have to be quick. You're in the basement of The Parker, and you've been unconscious nearly twenty minutes. Your hands are tied behind your back, but your legs are free. The Children of Iblis are down here with us. Two women, two men, and a teenage boy. One of them is a policeman."

Emmet. Sorrow raked my heart.

"They're wiring the place with explosives," she went

on. "From what I can tell, they think some bloke named George Fagin has Solomon's ring, and they believe you know where he is. They're going to make you tell them everything. And unless they get the ring, they'll blow the building up with us inside."

"They can't have it." My voice was a bare whisper.

"What's that?"

"They can't have the ring."

Her eyes widened. "You know where it is?"

I nodded until a fresh slice of pain made me stop.

"Scarlett, your little girl's here," Nuala said.

"Gemma—please tell me she's okay...."

"She's on the ground five feet behind you," Nuala said. "If you don't tell them where Fagin is, she'll die with us. And they'll go after your sister, too."

I heard Gemma's muffled whimper. Asked Nuala what had happened in the garage.

"They attacked as soon as I came out of the hospital," she said. "But that's not important now. You have to tell these people where the ring is."

"I don't have to tell them anything," I said, starting to work my wrists back and forth against whatever held them. "I don't need to."

"What do you mean?"

"I mean I have it. Here, with me."

Her face went rigid. The gold around her irises flashed in the naked light.

"You *brought* it?"

"Yeah," I said, remembering not to nod.

"My God, child, how could you? If they get their hands on that ring there'll be no stopping them. They'll restore their own powers and use the *Shubaak* to bring legions of jinn through to this world. Humans won't stand a chance!"

"I thought it was the only way I could keep Gemma alive. But I was wrong. They're going to blow us all up no matter what I do."

She shook her head. "Not if you'll let me help you."

"Please," I said, "roll me over so I can see Gemma."

"Tell me where the ring is. I'll hide it from them."

"Come closer," I said.

She did.

Gemma whimpered again, only louder.

"It's in my left front pocket."

"That's a love."

Nuala reached with her bound hands, found the signet ring, studied it. Then her eyes clouded over, green and black like a tornado sky.

"This can't be Solomon's ring. It has no seal, no adornment at all."

"Fagin filed the seal off to disguise it," I said. "But that's it, all right. The magic's still there."

She looked from the ring to me and back again. "It *is* heavy, like the legend says," she whispered, rolling the gold's weight around her palm. "But how can we be sure?"

"Hide it," I said. "We'll only use it for a bargaining chip if we have to. Put it…"

"*Shh!*" She shoved the ring into a pocket of her own. "They're coming."

"What's going on over here?" Blondie's sly hiss slithered across the concrete like an asp.

"We're deciding how long we should let you keep your teeth," I said. The binding on my wrists was starting to give. Barely.

She laughed and came to a stop in front of me. Oliver was behind her, along with Shorty and the Goon, Hashim. Oliver and Shorty looked overwhelmed. Hashim had a row of rough stitches along the gash I'd opened on his cheek, and a bandage around his forearm. I hoped that one was from Jones. He looked ready to kill me.

"Where's Fagin?" Blondie toed my leg with her boot.

"Why?" I said. "He doesn't have what you're looking for."

"What do you mean?"

"Go to hell."

She turned to Oliver. "Not very ladylike, is she?"

Oliver shook his head. Laughed nervously.

"Where's Emmet?" I said. "I want to see him so I can spit in his eye."

Blondie laughed, full and cruel.

"Oh, you poor thing! Feeling betrayed?"

Shorty smirked.

"Hash, bring over the policeman so Scarlett can tell him how naughty he's been."

Hashim would've preferred kicking in my face, but he trotted off like a good little henchman and came back, dragging Emmet's limp body by the heels.

Guilt and relief and anger shot through me all at once. Emmet hadn't betrayed me. He hadn't betrayed Reem. But he was hurt and unconscious and maybe even dead.

"Get the girl," Blondie snapped. Shorty scurried past me and came back with Gemma in her arms. Gemma wobbled when her feet hit the ground, then steadied.

Blondie ran a long, pale finger down Gemma's cheek. Gemma flinched. Her pants were stained where she'd wet herself. Over the cloth gag in her mouth, her eyes raced back and forth between Nuala and me. Tears streamed into the upturned goggles around her neck.

"Let her go or I won't tell you a goddamned thing," I said, working my wrists harder, ignoring the burn of raw skin and the first prickles of real panic.

"Oh no?" Blondie laughed. "Then let me tell *you* a few things. First, we found this."

Oliver held out the bottle from my backpack. The one I hadn't hidden in the drywall stacks earlier.

"We were never sure if the *Shubaak* we pried from your father's dead hands was real or not, but now we know it was a fake, just like the one we stole from the Library of Alexandria three months ago. You've had the real one all along."

I was running out of cards to play, and talking too much was only going to get someone hurt. So I kept my mouth shut.

Blondie bared her teeth in an ugly smile. "Cat got your tongue?"

I kept my mouth shut some more. Found even more play in the binding.

294

She walked over and kicked me in the solar plexus. "You'd do well to show more respect in the presence of Iblis, girl," she said.

I fought for air, told myself it would come once the spasms in my diaphragm let up.

Gemma whimpered again. Her eyes were frozen on Nuala. Nuala was leaning toward me.

"Scarlett?" She touched my cheek with one hand.

One.

Even deprived of oxygen, I knew her hands had been tied together.

There should have been two.

"You oughtn't have made things so difficult...."

No, no, no.

"...But you did. And now we have to do things the hard way."

I tried to yank a wrist loose. Couldn't do it. "You can't..."

"Oh," she purred, "but I can."

"It's you," I croaked. "You think you're Iblis."

A terrible smile spread across her lips. "I *know* I'm Iblis, love."

I heard an angry sob. Realized it was mine.

"And you?" Her top lip curled up in disdain. "Well,

let's just say it was a gorgeous stroke of luck that you came along when you did. It's almost like you were destined to help us. You've given us everything we lacked. That's why I kept you alive. Got you away from the *mu'aqqibat*. Helped you break free of your silly boyfriend at the hospital. You're a nuisance, love, but oh, so useful."

Blondie sneered. Oliver stared down at the floor.

"And look how my gamble has paid off!" Nuala said. "I spent years married to that old fool, Manny, thinking he was the only one who could lead me to the ring. But in just a few days, you've brought us the real *Shubaak* and the ring, both. In return, I'm going to let you live long enough to witness their power. And if you're especially good, I might even let you watch your friends die before I give you to Hashim."

She turned to Hashim.

"Get her up. And if you disobey me again like you did earlier, I'll kill you myself."

Hashim dropped his chin, guilty as a wayward first grader. Then he yanked me to my feet, gave my kidneys a jab. "That's a down payment," he growled.

"Hashim!" Nuala scolded.

"It was only a poke," he said.

Nuala smiled indulgently. "Yes, well, we've more important things to do before I let you have your fun. Much more important things." She slipped the signet ring onto her finger and snatched the bottle from Oliver's hands.

"I've waited so long," she whispered, running her fingers lovingly over the metal. "Ever since my father whispered stories of Solomon's betrayal to me at bedtime, telling me all that had been stolen from our ancestors, I've dreamed of returning my people to greatness. Now jinnkind will assume its rightful dominion over this miserable realm, and human blood will spill for a thousand years as penance for their sins against us."

The gold in her eyes threw off evil sparks.

"You're insane," I said.

Her hand shot out and slapped me. Gemma groaned and got a quick backhand of her own from Shorty.

Oliver flinched. "You said you wouldn't hurt my sister!"

"Shut up, fool," Nuala said, "and bear witness to the birth of my reign!"

She held up the *Shubaak*.

"It was so kind of Manny to explain that the lost

spell was never really lost, that it's been hidden in plain sight all these years...."

She knew. All the bearer of the ring had to do was hold the *Shubaak* and read the words written across it. And Nuala knew.

"We remain unvanquished!"

The words rang triumphantly across the basement. Nuala shuddered. Her beautiful face twisted into a smug mask of anticipation.

Everyone waited.

Nothing happened.

Nuala's eyes flew wide. "What have you done?" she snarled at me.

"Not a damn thing," I said. "Yet."

Quick as my rubbery muscles would let me, I bent my knees and jumped backward into the Goon's face. Bone gave way under the back of my head with a sickening crunch. Hashim went down, nose shattered, hands still gripping my shirt. I rolled with him until his hands went limp, then spun clear.

"Get her!" Nuala shrieked. Gemma kicked back into one of Shorty's knees, hitting at just the right angle to knock her kneecap sideways and bring her down.

Oliver rushed to his sister's side. I scrambled behind the nearest stack of drywall. Blondie was hot on my tail.

Even with my wrists tied, I was ready.

My shin flew high and hard enough to connect with her neck and drop her cold. She was unconscious before she hit the ground.

I staggered, wrenched to my right, and steadied myself against the drywall panels. The pile shifted, exposing the blackjack I'd stashed there earlier. That, and the real *Shubaak*, too.

Blondie twitched at my feet.

Hands still behind my back, I slid my thumb through Solomon's ring and yanked against the threads holding it to my jeans. The metal cut into my finger. I pulled harder. The stitches gave.

"Asha?" Shorty mewled from the other side of the stack.

"You mean Blondie?" I called back. "She's a little unconscious right now."

My blackjack sat on its shelf, begging to be used. I knew it was useless so long as my hands weren't free.

"But look how close she got to this."

I turned around and pushed my hands out past the

edge of the drywall, wiggling my fingers to show off Solomon's ring.

Nuala howled in frustration. "The true ring! Get it!"

I spun around. Got ready for Shorty or Oliver to come after me. Neither did.

"Asha!" Shorty wailed. "What have you done to Asha?"

I looked down at Blondie. She wasn't twitching anymore, but the shallow rise and fall of her chest told me she was still alive.

"Nothing she can't recover from," I said. "But I'll kill the both of you if you come back here."

I peeked out from behind the drywall. Shorty was on the ground, clutching her knee and staring stupidly up at Nuala. Oliver had planted himself in front of Gemma, shielding her. Nuala stood alone, her beauty gone. She was a thing of pure hate.

"Get her!" she barked at Shorty.

"Asha," Shorty sniffled.

Oliver pulled Gemma close.

On the floor behind Nuala, Emmet's eyes opened and found mine.

Alhamdulillah, I said under my breath. He was alive.

Fast as a cat, Nuala snatched Gemma away from

Oliver and pressed her forearm across the girl's throat. With her free hand, she took a small blowgun from a pouch at her waist and aimed it down at Shorty.

"Traitor," she said coldly. And blew.

Shorty's body seized. I watched, paralyzed, as her lips went blue and her fingers clawed at her throat. The agony went on forever. I thought of *Abbi*, of Decker, and focused on my own rage. There would be time enough for grief. Later.

Shorty jerked once. Twice. Finally went still.

Gemma let out a stifled wail. Nuala pulled a second dart and held it less than an inch from her neck.

With one last ripping tug, my right wrist slipped free. "You shouldn't have done that," I said.

"No?" Nuala glanced coldly at Shorty's corpse and smiled back at me.

Emmet was awake, trying to sit up. His holster was empty.

"You have the policeman's gun, Oliver," Nuala said. "Get the ring, or I'll kill your sister. It's that simple."

The nervous look in Oliver's eyes was shifting to desperation. He took the gun from the back of his pants. Gemma whimpered.

"Get. Me. The. Ring," Nuala said.

"You promised you wouldn't hurt Gemma," he said. "Let her go, then I'll help you."

"The *ring*, Oliver."

Oliver's chin trembled. He lifted the gun, let it drop, as if the weight of it were too much.

"She's lying," I said. "If she gets the ring, she'll kill us all and blow this place sky high."

"Shut up!" Nuala screamed. "Or I *will* kill the girl. And once I've taken the ring from you myself, I'll slit your fekkin' belly and leave you to die in a pool of your own intestines."

Oliver shuddered. Lifted the gun toward Nuala with both hands.

"What are you doing, fool?" Nuala snapped.

Gemma wept silently, too terrified to make a sound. Oliver's hands shook.

He's going to hit Gemma, I thought. Panic lit up my brain. Then, like lost hope found, *Abbi*'s words came to me: *Sheherazade refused to let anyone write her story for her. And you must do the same.*

My words, once I'd found them, were calm. Certain. Because I knew they were true.

"It's going to be okay, Oliver."

Emmet reached for his leg.

I stepped out from behind the drywall stack.

"Iblis?"

Nuala looked at me, saw the *Shubaak* in my hand. The dart at Gemma's neck wavered.

"The *Shubaak*," she whispered.

"That's right," I said. "The real one. *And* the ring."

"Open the portal." She pressed the dart to Gemma's skin. Gemma breathed fast and shallow.

"I can't," I told her.

"Open it. Or the girl dies."

Oliver's finger pressed against the trigger. The gun was going to fire, whether he meant it to or not.

"All right," I said. Oliver's finger relaxed. Nuala's hand did not.

"Say it," Nuala growled.

I swallowed hard. Closed my eyes.

"We."

My voice trembled.

Oliver turned to watch me. The gun's barrel lifted, pointing up to the concrete ceiling.

"Remain."

Nuala's lips parted. Her eyes glowed with hellish intensity. The dart's tip pulled away from Gemma's skin.

Emmet sat up behind her.

"Un—"

His knife hit Nuala's back before the word was done. She lurched forward. Her grip on Gemma loosened. Gemma crumpled to the floor.

"Emmet!" I shouted. He was already up, tackling Nuala's swaying body to the ground. The dart flew from her hand and skidded across the floor toward me. I kicked it behind the drywall. Nuala let out a choked gasp. Coughed a faint spray of blood onto the concrete. Didn't cough anymore.

Oliver hesitated, unsure what to do.

"You don't need that anymore, Oliver," I said.

His arm dropped. His face went slack.

"You saved your sister," I said, walking toward him. Gently, I tugged at the gun. Felt it slip from his fingers. "You saved her, Oliver."

He dropped to his knees. Drew Gemma stiffly into his arms. Her body folded into his. His own rigid limbs thawed. And then he was cradling her, the dampness of his own tears mingling with hers.

"I'm so sorry, Gemma," he whispered into her hair. "I'm so, so sorry."

Emmet shuffled toward me across the concrete. Every step looked like it hurt.

"What the hell just happened, Scarlett?" he said. "And what was that you were about to say?"

I smiled, caught up in the sight of Gemma getting her brother back.

"Scarlett?"

I leaned against Emmet's chest, grateful for the feel of something true.

"Unconvinced, Emmet. *I*. Remain. Unconvinced."

"What?"

"It's a long story," I said, relaxing for the first time since Gemma had walked into my office. "But I promise, once we get this mess cleaned up, I'll tell you the whole thing myself."

31

Rain was falling again on Carroll Street when Decker walked into my office a week later. His face was too pale against his dark gray turtleneck, but other than that, he looked like everything that was right with the world.

"Gingerbread scones," he said, setting a white paper bag on my desk alongside two cups of something that smelled suspiciously like coffee. "I gave some to Mook, too. He was cheery as ever."

I put the *Shubaak* back in my desk drawer and closed it a little too hard. Mook was still a tender subject.

"Whatcha up to?" Deck asked.

"Thinking how I'm kind of looking forward to prayers with Reem this Friday."

He grinned and walked to the couch. Jones lifted her head to sniff his hand.

"No hard feelings, old lady?" he asked.

Her stump of a tail thumped the cushion. He scratched behind her ears. She groaned happily and dropped her head.

"You're lucky, Deck," I said. "If I were her, I don't know if I'd forgive you for wanting to let me die."

"We all make mistakes," he said, coming back to my client chair. "Speaking of which, what happened with the homeless guy from the garage? Did he give a statement to Emmet after all?"

"Christopher?" I said. "He did, even though seeing Nuala attack you scared him half to death. And even though he's never had what you'd call an easy relationship with cops. Lucky for us, he'd do anything for Reem."

"Well, I'm grateful for that. And for him taking care of Jones, too. That security guard, Dimitri, knew she was in the back of the truck, but he stayed with me until Ma showed up and then got tied up filing reports. Jones probably would have died if it weren't for Christopher."

I looked over at my dog.

"Do you think Delilah would mind leaving a collection jar out at the diner for Christopher?" I asked. "Reem talked him into rehab, but he'll need help after he gets out."

Deck took the lid off his coffee and sipped at it. Too much cream, too much sugar. I could tell from the color. Mine was black, no sugar. Just right.

"She already put out two—one for him, one for Dimitri. And she's making damn sure they fill up fast."

The thought of Delilah tapping her foot and blocking the door until every customer put change in the jars made me laugh.

"What about Gemma?" Deck asked. "How's she doing?"

"She's a tough kid," I said. "She'll be fine. And her parents have Oliver in therapy with some shrink Emmet recommended. I'm trying to get Sam Johnson to go to the same lady; he's got some heavy stuff to deal with. We'll see."

I drank some coffee. Took out a scone.

"Your turn," I said. "Tell me about Manny and Sister. How'd their meeting go?"

"Well," Deck said with a wicked grin. "It went well."

"Yeah?"

"Yeah. They talked for hours over this huge meal

Manny cooked for her. He told her all about the ring, and she told him about her business. She said it was a relief to know the ring was back where it belonged. He's still hurting over Nuala, but I have a feeling Sister Lillian George Fagin might just be able to help him out with that."

It was an odd pairing—a Muslim tattoo artist and a billionaire nun who wasn't really a nun. But the more I thought about it, the more I liked it.

Jones snored lightly. Rain pattered down. My office was warm and smelled like a bakery.

"This is nice," Deck said.

"It is." I looked out the window at the General sipping coffee of his own in the doorway where Blondie had stalked me. She was in jail now, and that was a good thing. So was Hashim. Nuala and Shorty were dead.

And Reem knew everything. She'd listened, dry-eyed and quiet, until my tale was told out. Then both of us had cried, together, until there were no tears left. After that, we'd called Emmet, cooked a meal that would have made *Ummi* proud, and sat down at the table to go through the whole story one more time.

The General waved up at me. I waved back.

Decker stood and walked around to my side of the desk. Took the coffee from my hand. Set it down.

"Come here," he said, pulling me up. He moved us away from the window and out of the General's sight. Out of everyone's sight.

"Are you ready to show me that tattoo yet?"

"No way," I said. "It's *haraam* enough, me being here with you alone."

"You gave up the right to use that one when you got the tattoo," he laughed, pressing his palm against my chest. Underneath it was a small indigo knot. And underneath that was my heart.

His lips floated over the skin of my neck, so soft I didn't want to breathe.

"I still can't believe Manny agreed to do it," I said.

"I still can't believe you're praying five times a day." He slid one of his fingers down my spine.

"I guess now that I've solved *Abbi*'s murder, I need something more," I said.

His hair brushed my chin as he nodded in agreement.

"Deck?" My voice was barely a whisper.

He lifted his head, stared into my eyes like they were the only place in the world.

"What, Scarlett?"

"Kiss me," I whispered against the sound of the rain.

And he did.

Acknowledgments

Giving credit to everybody who had a hand in shaping Scarlett would mean working forward from my second-grade teacher, Mrs. Tietze, who let us spend Fridays after lunch filling up our story notebooks. That was a long. Time. Ago. So I'm going to skip ahead a lot of years and miss a lot of people. To all those neglected souls, if you think you had a hand in making my brain need to tell stories, you're probably right. I owe you.

Okay—here goes:

I love you, Mom. Thank you.

Thank you, Sean (embarrassing pet name withheld—you're welcome), for knowing I could. And thank you, Zoomie and Sophie Bean (embarrassing pet names not withheld—you're welcome), for putting up with my chronic Disappearing Mom Syndrome and grouchy revising days.

Shai Kaiser and Ann Savage, you guys were my very

first readers. You were in eighth grade then, and you're literally graduating high school as I type this now. I miss you both and know you're going to do amazing things.

Rachel Orr, I owe you so much for seeing something in my writing that was apparently there after all. Thank you for sticking with me through a whole lot of drafts and "Did you hear anything yet?" e-mails. And thank you, Pam Garfinkel, for being such a thoughtful, encouraging, flat-out wonderful editor. You rock.

Muchísimas gracias, Alvina Ling, for recognizing potential in a very early version of this book and suggesting that I get rid of the Valkyrie…and the banshee. And thank you, Christine Ma, for doing such a fabulous job making sure my *i*'s were dotted and my *t*'s were crossed.

Finally, I'm grateful to Omer Kazmi for trying his level best to help me, not just with Arabic, but also with portraying Islam and Arabic culture accurately and sensitively. Any failures on that front are both entirely mine and entirely unintentional. In the end, though, the world's a complicated place, and characters like Scarlett don't always behave. Plus, as we've already established, I'm stubborn. And I don't always listen.

Just like Scarlett.

Turn the page for a sneak peek of
Jennifer Latham's *Dreamland Burning*.

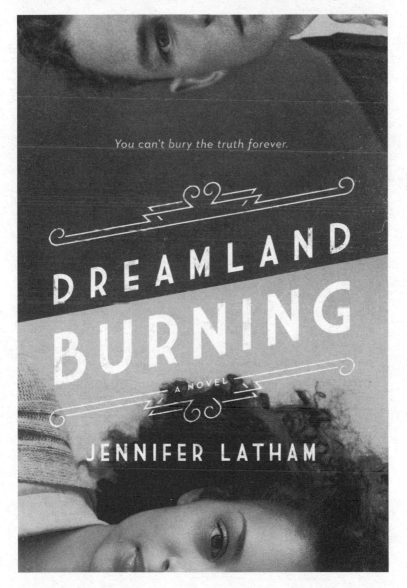

Rowan

Nobody walks in Tulsa. At least not to get anywhere. Oil built our houses, paved our streets, and turned us from a cow town stop on the Frisco Railroad into the heart of Route 66. My ninth-grade Oklahoma History teacher joked that around these parts, walking is sacrilege. Real Tulsans drive.

But today my car is totaled and I have an eleven-thirty appointment with the district attorney at the county courthouse. So I walked.

Mom and Dad wanted to come home and pick me up after their morning meetings. I convinced them the walk would help me clear my head, and it did. Especially when I got to the place where he died.

Honestly, I'd been a little worried that being there again would mess me up. So to keep myself calm, I imagined how things must have looked the night Will and

Joseph and Ruby tried to survive. There's this old map of Tulsa online, and the streets I walked along to get here are on it. In 1921, the Arkansas River cut them off to the south, just like it does today. But back then they ran north into trees and fields and farms. There aren't any farms now, only highways and concrete.

It was probably quieter a hundred years ago, but that doesn't necessarily mean better. I understand now that history only moves forward in a straight line when we learn from it. Otherwise it loops past the same mistakes over and over again.

That's why I'm here, wearing one of Mom's knee-length business skirts, sitting on a bench near the courthouse, waiting to tell the DA what happened. I want to stop just one of those loops. Because it's like Geneva says: The dead always have stories to tell. They just need the living to listen.

———

Everything started the first Monday of summer vacation. It was my only chance at a real day off, because the next morning I was supposed to start the internship Mom had arranged. It was the kind of thing that would look good on college applications and get me recommendation letters from people with *MD* after their names. I didn't especially want to be locked up in a sterilized research lab all summer, but I never bothered to look for something better. The way things stood, I had one day all my own to sleep late, eat Nutella with a spoon, and send James a thousand texts about nothing.

Only I didn't get to do any of that.

At 7 AM on the dot, a construction crew pulled into the driveway and started slamming truck doors and banging tools around. Hundred-year-old windows do a crap job of keeping things out, so even though the men spoke quietly, I could hear their murmurs and smell the smoke from their cigarettes.

After a while, the side gate squeaked open and the guys carried their tools to the servants' quarters behind our house. Just so you don't get the wrong idea, that sounds a lot more impressive than it is. I mean, yes, we have money, but no one in my family has had live-in servants since my great-great-grandparents. After they died, my great-uncle Chotch moved into the back house. Years earlier, when Chotch was two, he'd wandered out of the kitchen and fallen into the pool. By the time the gardener found him and got him breathing again, he was blue and brain-damaged. He'd lived, though, and was good at cutting hair. Dad says he gave free trims to all the workers at the oil company my great-great-grandfather founded, right up until the day he died. That was in 1959.

The only things living in the back house since then have been holiday decorations, old furniture, Uncle Chotch's Victrola, and termites. Then, last Christmas, Mom decided that even though there are three unused bedrooms in the main house, we needed a guest cottage, too.

Dad fought her on it, I think because he's a nice liberal white guy weirded out by the idea that the back house was built for black servants. If it had been up to him, he would have let it rot.

Mom was not okay with that.

Her great-grandfather had been the son of a maid, raised in the back house of a mansion two blocks over. He'd gone on to graduate first in his class from Morehouse College and become one of Tulsa's best-known black attorneys. Mom went to law school to carry on the family legal tradition and ended up *owning* a back house. For her, it mattered.

"I won't stand by and let a perfectly good building crumble to dust," she'd argued. There had been some closed-door negotiations between her and Dad after that, then a few days where they didn't talk to each other at all. In the end, Dad started referring to the back house as his "man cave," and while he shopped for gaming systems and a pool table, Mom interviewed contractors.

That was six months ago. The renovations started in May.

I lay there listening to the workmen's saw, figuring I had maybe three minutes before our grumpy neighbor, Mr. Metzidakis, started banging on the front door to complain about the noise.

Only he didn't have to.

The saw stopped on its own. The gate creaked open.

Equipment clunked against the truck bed. And the men talked so fast and low that I could only catch four words.

Huesos viejos. Policía. Asesinato.

Which, yes, I understood—thank you, Señora Markowitz and tres años de español. And which, yes, was enough to get me out of bed and over to the window in time to see their truck back out onto the street and drive away.

Something strange was going on, and I wanted to know what. So I snagged a pair of flip-flops and headed for the back house.

It was a disaster inside. A week before, the workmen had demolished the ceiling and pulled all the toxic asbestos insulation. After that, they'd hacked out big chunks of termite-tunneled plaster from the walls and ripped the old Formica countertops off the cabinets. A gritty layer of construction dust coated everything, including Uncle Chotch's old Victrola in the corner. *At least they covered it with plastic*, I thought, stepping around boxes of tile and grout on my way to the fresh-cut hole in the floor at the back of the room.

Only once I got there, I forgot about the Victrola completely and understood exactly what had sent the workmen running.

Huesos viejos. Policía. Asesinato.

Old bones.

Police.

Murder.

WILLIAM

I wasn't good when the trouble started. Wasn't particularly bad, either, but I had potential. See, Tulsa in 1921 was a town where boys like me roamed wild. Prohibition made Choctaw beer and corn whiskey more tempting than ever, and booze wasn't near the worst vice available.

My friend Cletus Hayes grew up in a house two doors down from mine. His father was a bank executive muckety-muck with a brand-new Cadillac automobile and friends on the city council. For that reason alone, Mama and Pop generally let Clete's knack for mischief slide. He and I got along fine eighty percent of the time, and kept each other's company accordingly.

One thing we always did agree on was that misbehaving was best done in pairs. Plenty of the roustabout gangs running Tulsa's streets would have taken us in, but I always figured the two of us were spoiled enough and maybe even smart enough to know the difference between hell-raising and causing real harm. Those gangs were chock-full of unemployed young men back from the Great War who'd come to Oklahoma looking for oilfield work down at the Glenn Pool strike. They'd seen bad things, done a few themselves, and liked showing off for locals. Problem was, the locals would try to one-up 'em, the roustabouts would take things a step further, and in the end, someone always spent the night in jail. That's why Clete and me kept to ourselves. We weren't angels, but we weren't hardened or hollow, either. Of course, even fair-to-middling boys like us veered off the righteous path from time to time. Some worse than others.

I was only seventeen, but had the shoulders and five-o'clock shadow of a full-grown man. More than one girl at Tulsa Central High School had her eye on me, and that's the truth. None of them stood a chance, though; Adeline Dobbs had stolen my heart way back in second grade, and the fact that she was a year older and the prettiest girl in school didn't dampen my hopes of winning her in the least.

She was a beauty, Addie was; slim and graceful as prairie grass, with black hair and eyes like a summer sky. I dreamed about that girl, about her clean smell and the peek of her lashes underneath her hat brim. And I loved her for her kindness, too. Boys followed her about like pups, but she always managed to deflect their affections without wounding their pride.

For years I loved her from afar, and spent no small amount of energy convincing myself it was only a matter of time before she started loving me back. Maybe that's why what happened at the Two-Knock Inn that cool March night tore me up so bad.

I was on my third glass of Choc and feeling fine when Addie arrived. Clete was there, too, dancing with a pretty, brown-skinned girl. For when it came to the fairer sex, a sweet smile and a pair of shapely legs were all it took to turn him colorblind. Not that it mattered at the Two-Knock. Jim Crow laws may have kept Negroes and whites separated in proper Tulsa establishments, but in juke joints and speakeasies out on the edge of town, folks didn't care about your skin color near so much as they did the contents of your wallet.

The Two-Knock was a rough place, though. A place where girls like Addie didn't belong. Even so, the sight of her coming through that door took my breath away. She was a vision: crimson dress, lips painted to match, eyes all wild and bright. Clete saw her, too, and made his way to my side after the song ended and poked me in the ribs, saying, "Lookee who just walked in!"

I didn't have breath enough to respond, so Clete jabbed me again. Said, "What're you waiting for, Will? Go talk to her!"

I wanted to. Lord, how I wanted to. But Addie was too good for the Two-Knock, and I couldn't quite reconcile myself with her being there.

When I didn't move, Clete rolled his eyes and socked me on the shoulder. Said, "This is it, dummy! If you don't go over and buy her a drink, you're the biggest jackass I know."

To which I replied that Addie didn't drink. And Clete snorted, "We're in a speakeasy, knucklehead. She didn't come for tea."

I shrugged. Signaled the bartender for another glass of Choc and slugged most of it down soon as it arrived. Then I looked back at Addie and asked Clete if he really thought I should go over.

"Hell yes!" he said.

So I puffed up my chest like the big dumb pigeon I was and got to my feet. Which was when the front door opened, and everything changed.

The man who walked in was tall and handsome, muscled all over, and browner than boot leather. Something about him shone. Drew your eyes like he was the one thing in the world worth looking at. *He* only had eyes for Addie, though, and she gave him a smile like sunrise when he sat down beside her.

I dropped back onto the barstool.

"You better chase him off," Clete said. But my throat was tight, and I only just managed to mumble, "Nothin' I can do."

"You kiddin' me?" he said. "That boy's out of line!"

I stayed quiet and stared at Addie's pale hand perched atop the table. She and the man were talking. Smiling.

Laughing. With every word, his fingers moved closer to hers.

Hate balled up inside me like a brass-knuckled fist. And when he slowly, slowly ran his fingertip across her skin, every foul emotion in the world churned deep down in the depths of my belly. Glancing sideways at a white woman was near enough to get Negroes lynched in Tulsa. Shot, even, in the middle of Main Street at noon, and with no more consequence than a wink and a nudge and a slap on the back. And God help me, that's exactly what I wanted for the man touching my Addie.

I wanted him dead.

About the Author

Jennifer Latham is an army brat with a soft spot for babies, books, and poorly behaved dogs. She's the author of *Scarlett Undercover* and *Dreamland Burning* and lives in Tulsa, Oklahoma, with her husband and two daughters.